AF506882

Skulls in the Shadows

D. Leitrim

SKULLS IN THE SHADOWS

ISBN: 979-8-9916742-0-1 (trade paperback)

First edition: October 2024

FOR MY UNCLE, J.F.

PROLOGUE

Hypnotic mind control was developed by the occultists of western Europe during the Renaissance. The hypnotic control system combined polyphonic voice commands with occult hieroglyphs and, when combined with the *Jomhuri-ye Eslâmi-ye* Talisman of Persian mystics, was irresistible.

Mind control was declared heresy by Pope Leo XIII and erased from history.

In 1942, the dark magick spell-casters of the Axis powers re-discovered the mesmerism system of the erased occultists. The Axis created a mind-controlling living weapon which they hoped would turn the tide of the losing war.

DURING THE ENLIGHTENMENT, THE TRIPLE KINGDOM OF Sardincia's addictive and mildly hallucinogenic Kanna-kannack tobacco became a lucrative cash crop.

In 1796, Pope Pious VI declared the Kannakannack tobacco to be Satanic in nature, and trade with Sardincia was banned.

The Triple Kingdom of Sardincia became an isolated and poverty-stricken country.

DURING WORLD WAR II, THE CAUDILLO OF SPAIN READ his spies' reports about occult super-soldiers. Terrified by the occult, the dictator set up Division M of the Social Investigation Brigade. The dictator gave his brigade the authority to brutally enforce draconian anti-occult laws in his country.

CHAPTER 1

In 1942, Axis bombs turned the city of El Alamein into a scorched and pitted hellscape. Jacques Proust and his squad took cover in what was thought to be a bomb-proof bunker. As the twelve men huddled in the concrete room and prayed to survive the night, an explosion blew the bunker's metal door from its hinges.

The door's flight ended with a crash when it hit the bunker's far wall. Jacques and the rest of the men aimed their guns at the open aperture, prepared to fight the stream of enemy soldiers they assumed would spew into the bunker.

Jacques watched the doorway and saw impossibly thin, pale, long, hairless fingers reach around the door-jam. The fingers moved as if attached to a being that found human interaction more terrifying than the El Alamein battlefield outside.

The fingers and hands stretched into a "Don't shoot, I surrender!" gesture, followed by two human arms.

Jacques and the rest of the men shouted, "Get in! Get the !*$*$*&# in!" The men didn't scream encouragement because they cared about whoever was at the door. They screamed because they were terrified that whatever was at the door would give the presence of the bunker away.

The thin, shell-shocked creature that might have once been a human overcame its fear and peered into the bunker. Another large explosion burst on the battlefield outside, and the creature that had once been a human scurried into the bunker like a huge spider with four limbs.

The spider-type man scurried to the far side of the bunker, nestled itself between two of Jacques' squad members, and whispered something Jacques couldn't hear. The squad members, Private Thomas and Private Krebs, grabbed the scurrying man, then hissed "Get Away!" and threw the scurrying thing to Jacques' side of the bunker.

Jacques got a good look at the thing which had survived the deadly no man's land of the El Alamein battlefield. The man was impossibly tall and thin and cowered like a beat dog. Tattoos on his torso peeked out from under his uniform's collar.

Jacques heard the creature mutter, "He's coming. Hide.

Don't look! Don't Listen!" The words sounded like the blubbering of a toddler.

Then Jacques heard a command being shouted into the bunker, "Do it! Do it, you bastard!"

A pained expression came over the face of the thin creature, and the creature's eyes rolled back in its head. Then Jacques heard the humming.

The humming from the creature the Axis forces called the *die schädel* permeated every inch of Jacques, as well as every other Allied soldier in the bunker. Jacques realized he couldn't move. From his prone position, Jacques could see the bunker doorway. Two Axis soldiers stood there.

The first soldier wore the insignia of an Axis sergeant. The sergeant stood in the broken doorway, a look of disgust on face. The second soldier was a private, a terrified expression on his face, a cigarette hanging from his mouth. The second soldier cradled a satchel, holding the leather bag as if it contained fine china.

An explosion rocked the outside of the bunker, and the enemy sergeant scurried inside. The satchel-carrying second man disappeared from view.

Once in the room, the Sergeant hissed, "*Schädel!* Order them! Order them out of this bunker! I am Sergeant Ording, your superior, and I order you to do this!"

The creature continued to hum, but none of the Allied soldiers moved.

Sergeant Ording shuffled across the room to the creature, the hurried shuffle of a man who couldn't believe his orders hadn't been obeyed even before he gave them. Sergeant Ording shouted over his soldier to the Axis private who had been in the doorway, "Private Braun! Get in here!" but Private Berhtram Braun was nowhere to be seen.

Ording realized that his human back-up was probably dead. He started to howl commands, then hiss threats, then throw insults at the humming creature, the Allied soldiers, and the Allied soldier's mothers. None of the soldiers moved.

Frustration boiling through him, Ording turned to the *die schädel* and hissed, "Do it."

The creature cowered against the wall next to Jacques, whimpering.

Ording hissed again, "Do it!"

The creature turned to the center of the room. With a pained look on his face, the creature hissed at the twelve soldiers in the room. Jacques tried to raise his arm to shoot the sergeant or the creature, but couldn't.

The creature lunged towards Private Thomas, grabbed Thomas by his uniform's collar, stared into the eyes of the soldier, and growled a command. Private Thomas took his weapon, ran through the small bunker opening, and charged into the field. The remaining men in the bunker heard the charging soldier's screams as he was cut down by a hail of bullets.

Jacques watched as the *die schädel* used his occult hypnotic powers on the next man. One by one, the creature commanded each soldier to charge to the battlefield and to death. By the end of the slaughter, only Jacques, the *die schädel* creature, and Ording remained.

As explosions shook the walls of the bunker, Jacques swore that no matter what happened, he wouldn't be like the others, that he wouldn't fall to the creature's mental commands. Then Jacques realized the humming had gotten much, much stronger.

The humming was like the sounds of a thousand bees and it shook Jacques to his bones. Jacques couldn't move, but he could feel the hands of the creature grasping both sides of his face.

The creature stared into Jacques' eyes. The humming Jacques heard was replaced by a command. "Run. Go Run! Run into the battlefield!"

All desire to stay in the bunker left Jacques. He gripped his weapon, stood up, and ran to the entrance of the bunker, ready to go fight and die.

Before Jacques made it to the entrance of the bunker, the bullet-riddled body of Private Thomas crawled to the entrance of the bunker from the outside. By instinct, Jacques ducked to one side when he saw the barrel of a Lee-Enfield rifle being pointed in his direction.

As Jacques ducked, Private Thomas pulled the trigger on his weapon, firing the ten rounds in his magazine into the *die schädel* creature. As Private Thomas fired, Ording screamed, "No! No! No!"

The bullets ripped into the seven-foot-tall disfigured man and the humming that controlled Jacques stopped. Jacques heard Ording hiss, "You bastard!"

Ording's words were drowned out by a screeching of a plane from outside the bunker. Bullets from a Focke-Wulf FW 190 tore Private Thomas apart. Jacques knew he had seconds to move before the Dornier bomber—the bomber that always followed the path cleared by the Focke-Wulf fighters—dropped its bombs.

Jacques dived to the far corner of the bunker. Ording ran to the front of the bunker, screaming up to the sky, "No! No! No! I am still here!"

As Jacques heard the Axis agent scream, the Allied soldier said a prayer for safety. Jacques heard a huge explosion before losing consciousness.

Jacques woke up days later in a British hospital, recovering from his wounds. Jacques' doctors believed his story of an Axis Sergeant and nearly seven-foot-tall private with hypnotic powers to be a panic-induced fantasy.

As the doctors told Jacques to rest, he knew the Sergeant and the strange creature were real.

Chapter 2

In September 1943, Axis warplanes bombed London.

Thadeus Martin had been sent to Britain weeks earlier, as Thadeus' mother believed Britain to be safer than Paris. Thadeus imagined the trip would be a furlough from school that had only two drawbacks. The first was that his wealthy and eccentric aunt would insist that he learn Spanish. The second was that the weeks in England were weeks away from his Mary, his crush.

When the rumors spread in London that an Axis bombing campaign against civilians was imminent, Thadeus and his aunt received a form letter assuring all residents that any and all bombing rumors were baseless. Also in the envelope were orders on how and when to queue for entrance to the newly constructed London bomb shelters, as "even though rumors of a bombing were baseless, precautions must be followed."

The shelter was a subway station—a yards-long underground tunnel reached by a winding staircase. The tracks and platform of the station had been covered with plywood. Sawhorses with 4x4 boards laid across created seating. Drapery had been set up at the mouths and on the walls of the tunnel. As the British women, children, and old men filed into the station, none of them asked, "Do drapes and park benches convert a tunnel into a shelter?"

At the bottom of the winding staircase that led to the station platform, Thadeus' aunt miraculously got herself and the young Thadeus a seat near her pastor.

Pastor Edmon was a charismatic senior citizen who wore eye-glasses that resembled the bottom of coke bottles, boasted continually of his time in the Great War, and predicted the Axis would be swiftly defeated. It was Pastor Edmon who was the unofficial leader of the group in the tunnel, the man who quietly mentioned that "Things in our current situation may be less than bright, but think of the challenges the boys in the field have."

When the door to the shelter was locked and the generator that provided light to the tunnel was shut off, it was Pastor Edmon who broke the news both times. "Now, now," proclaimed the Pastor, "The door is shut, just like we shut the door to our homes every night. Nothing to be concerned about. The lights? Nothing to be concerned about. Gasoline rationing is all it is! We have darkness every night, and candles to fight off the darkness tonight. Just like on one's birthday."

In the first hour of the night, as the candles were lit and passed to the residents of the shelter, the Pastor's booming voice filled the tunnel, and his prayers thanked the Lord in advance for military victory.

The crowd in the tunnel lost track of time. The darkness and boredom made every minute seem like an hour. The old men kept their pocket-watches closed so they wouldn't see the minute-hand creep by. Women put out their candles in the hope of getting some sleep. The Pastor stopped leading the group in prayer, and the tunnel became silent. In the silence, Thadeus heard a soft humming.

Thadeus looked around, wanting to see if anyone else had heard what he'd heard. No one made eye contact. Because of his ear infection, the humming caused a sharp and slight pain in Thadeus' ear.

A huge explosion shook the tunnel. A few soft "Ohs" escaped the lips of the crowd, and everyone realized the bombing had started. The Pastor's voice boomed once again as Edmon filled the tunnel with prayers that thanked the Lord in advance for military victory. Thadeus recognized the hint of fear that had entered the Pastor's voice.

Thadeus heard the humming. Not wanting the others in the tunnel to think he was losing his mind, Thadeus said nothing.

In the second hour, Thadeus noticed the Pastor's booming prayer of thanks for victory changed to whispered prayer pleading for victory. In the second hour, people realized their homes were destroyed, that the tunnel would be their home for the rest of the war. In the second hour stronger bombs shook dirt and tiles and timber and concrete loose from the tunnel's ceiling and walls. Thadeus heard people in the crowd whisper, "This is worse than what I thought it would be."

In the second hour, Thadeus not only heard, but felt the humming. As the bombs fell and the tunnel shook, the humming got louder and louder and stronger and stronger. Thadeus felt the vibration under his skin, in his bones. The pain got worse. Still, he said nothing. *It's just the bombs. The stress of the darkness and the shaking. If I ignore it, it will go away.*

At the start of the third hour, there was a pause in the bombing and the Pastor screamed in relief, "It's over! It's finally over!" At that moment, a deafening explosion filled the air of the shelter and the walls shook with such ferocity that even the most unemotional of the English whispered, "Oh God."

The Pastor cried out, "Oh Lord Jesus!"

After the huge explosion, a torrent of debris that left inches of dirt on the women and children fell into the tunnel. There was a shaking where all the residents of the shelter assumed they were dead. Then there was an unexpected quiet, and all that was heard was the quiet sobbing of Pastor Edmon. The residents of the shelter tactfully ignored the soft sobbing of their leader.

Thadeus was the only person to notice a soft ripple in the curtains at the far end of the shelter.

The Pastor stopped crying. Every one of the civilians welcomed the silence and didn't question why they should be graced by stillness, a stillness not rocked by bombs or emotion. Emotional and physically exhausted, taking advantage of the quiet, the civilians fell into slumber. Everyone slept, except Thadeus.

As Thadeus lay motionless next to his aunt, his infected ear ringing, he heard a loud "Clunk!"—the sound of a large circuit breaker being thrown. A single strand of lights, at the very zenith of the tunnel, turned on.

In the flickering shadows caused by the dim new light, Thadeus saw a pair of impossibly long and thin arms appear from behind the curtain that covered the far end of the tunnel.

Fear crept into his soul as he saw the head and torso of a freakishly thin, seven-foot-tall, pale man crawl into the shelter from behind the curtain. The man crawled head first, scurrying like a huge spider, dressed in rags so tattered Thadeus couldn't determine if the uniform was Axis or Allies.

After the *die schädel* scurried into the room, he stopped and tilted his head. The creature sniffed the air, paused, sniffed again, then turned his head in the direction of Pastor Edmon. Edmon was drenched in sweat, his eyes clenched closed.

As the creature crawled through the sleeping crowd, Thadeus noticed the thing's uneven gait. *This thing is limping.*

The creature kept one arm close to his torso.

This monster is hurt.

Thadeus watched the thin thing shuffle the length of the tunnel, bumping and jostling the residents. After each bump, the *die schädel* would pause and lift his head as if trying to talk.

As the creature got nearer to Pastor Edmon, Thadeus realized, *He's not talking. The creature is humming. Or trying to hum.*

The creature had finally reached Pastor Edmon. Thadeus saw the strain on the face of the *die schädel*.

Thadeus tried to warn the Pastor, tried to raise his arm and say, "Pastor! Behind you!" but Thadeus' arm felt as if it was trapped beneath a fifty-pound sandbag.

Thadeus was distracted but the sound of quick,

determined footsteps echoing from down the hall. August Ording appeared from behind the same curtain the creature had appeared from behind minutes earlier.

Ording was dressed as a country laborer going to church. Work pants, back shirt, collar, all covered by a worn denim work-man's jacket.

The man had a gait of a fed-up parent—a parent who had had many talks with a poorly behaving son and was now walking into a rumpus room to have the same talk with the same unruly son one more time.

From the far end of the tunnel, Ording hissed to the creature, "Lead these cattle into the street."

Ording's order was loud and echoed through the tunnel, but woke none of the hypnotically asleep crowd. Ording's call didn't even get the attention of Pastor Edmon, who sat with his eyes clamped shut as Ording marched closer to him.

Thadeus didn't move. Thadeus barely breathed. He just told himself, *The man doesn't see me, he can't see me in the dim light.*

Thadeus watched Ording march through the sleeping crowd until he reached the feverishly mumbling, sweating, eyes-closed in concentration Pastor Edmon.

Ording walked to an arm's length of the creature and hissed the command, "Get this Holy Man to lead these people out of here! Into the street!" Ording sneered when he said "Holy man" as if the phrase made no sense.

The creature crawled to Edmon, grabbed the Pastor on either side of his head, and stared into Edmon's eyes.

Pastor Edmon struggled to stand and mumbled, "I think we should go."

Ording hissed, "You're going. Now!" The *die schädel* creature was humming, and Thadeus realized, *The slaughter of civilians. This is the type of victory the enemy wants.*

Edmon muttered, "If it's time to go, it's time to go." The Pastor got up and started to shuffle towards the stairs, leaving the creature behind. The other residents of the tunnel started to rise, as if sleep-walking, and followed Edmon.

The creature hissed something to Ording, and Ording hissed back, "We have time! We must make time!"

The creature hissed again, in some type of language just he and Ording spoke. Ording hissed back at the creature, "That doesn't matter! If we fail tonight, we are as good as dead anyway!"

The creature wheezed. Pastor Edmon started to lead his followers to the stairs.

Thadeus felt something pulling him, something willing himself to get up and walk outside. Thadeus' inner ear pounded in pain. He willed himself to stay still, to not move.

Ording squinted, the way a mechanic squints when he hears an engine make a noise it shouldn't.

Ording commanded his creature, "Keep at it." Then

Ording started to explore the tunnel, getting closer and closer to Thadeus.

The civilians had reached the bottom of the stairs and had started to file upwards towards the street.

Then the creature started to fidget like a dog that had been beaten too much and hissed something at Ording again.

Ording hissed back, "We have time!" And then, "What is that? Do you sense that? Try harder!"

The humming in the creature started to shake Thadeus' every cell. The pain in his infected ear caused his body to shake.

Thadeus saw his aunt get up and start to shuffle to the stairs. Thadeus found the will to shout, "Don't go! Auntie, don't go!"

Ording's head whipped towards Thadeus and screeched, "You!" Ording marched towards Thadeus, through the crowd.

Thadeus bellowed, "Stop! Stop!"

The creature stopped humming, like a confused dog when a trick goes bad. The crowd started to blink awake. Pastor Edmon, realizing he was on the stairs, commanded everyone, "Get back! Everyone, get back!"

The creature screeched a noise that was almost a word, a sound that was generated by pure fear.

Thadeus could hear the whistle of a bomb falling close

to the shelter. The shelter shook. As the roar of an explosion permeated the shelter, Thadeus screamed, felt the dirt falling from the ceiling, covering him.

Ording scream, "I curse you! I curse you!"

THADEUS WOKE UP TO THE FEELINGS OF HANDS, HUN-dreds of hands, all over his body. He heard a voice cry, "Boy! Boy! Stop it! We are digging you free!"

Thadeus opened his eyes and saw the silhouettes of men staring at him. Behind the silhouettes Thadeus saw open sky. He was alive.

The uniformed men were part of London's civil defense corps. Gaining his senses, Thadeus muttered, "Auntie?"

A member of the corps replied, "Everyone is fine, son. Everyone is fine."

Thadeus muttered, "There were saboteurs in the tunnel. A tall man, another that gives orders. Did you get them?"

One of Thadeus' rescuers, an older gentleman whose manner and uniform indicated he was a person in charge, spoke. "Some of the other victims mentioned two men like that. We didn't find them. Likely it's a case of mass hysteria. Best to forget the whole thing."

Thadeus wouldn't forget, especially Ording's last words, "I curse you."

Chapter 3

Roland O'Brien had heard a rumor the invasion would launch tomorrow morning. Unlike other Allied soldiers, Roland had no intention of running into battle.

On June 5, 1944, the Allied Army was stationed on the Weymouth fields, past the Weymouth Forest, at the literal edge of England. The rows and rows of tents on the acres of grass housed thousands of American, British, and Canadian soldiers. The camp was silent as each soldier tried to get a night's sleep, eager to be deployed into battle.

Roland stood hidden at the edge of the Weymouth Forest and glared over the Weymouth Cliffs, across the English Channel, in the direction of France. Staring into that darkness above the roiling waves, Roland pictured the

Axis army on the opposite side of the waterway.

"When they get the order, thousands of these saps are going to run up that beach into France, right into the bullets of the Axis machine-gunners," Roland muttered to himself. "To blazes with that. Roland O'Brien doesn't take a bullet in the guts for anyone."

Roland tightly gripped the amulet he held in his hand. Feeling the weight of the ancient artifact, Roland muttered to himself, "Roland O'Brien isn't a sap. You, my beautiful little medallion, are going to make sure I don't get shot tomorrow."

Since his enlistment, Roland O'Brien had become a wealthy man. O'Brien had made his money by selling smuggled cheap booze, stolen Red Cross sleeping pills, and adult magazines to desperate privates at insanely high prices. The immoral criminal in the Allied forces had done very well for himself and was looking for a way to keep the good times rolling.

The Axis criminal network, as rife with traitors as their Allied criminal counterparts, had contacted their peers on the Allied side. The Axis criminals let the Allied smugglers know that whoever could get a certain mystic artifact from the British Royal Museum would be spared during the upcoming battle.

Using the money his illegal activities had earned, Roland employed the best breaking and entering specialists in London. The amulet of *Jomhuri-ye Eslâmi-ye* was stolen from the British Royal Museum and delivered to him.

Roland planned to give the *Jomhuri-ye Eslâmi-ye* amulet to the Axis forces in exchange for safe passage through the battlefields of war. Being a back-stabber and thief himself, he knew that whoever the Axis sent might kill him and rob him of the *Jomhuri-ye Eslâmi-ye*. Roland glanced over his shoulder and checked to see if his crime-partner, the alcoholic supply sergeant Pete Kolems, was nearby.

Pete had been Roland's second in command in various smuggling operations and had shown his loyalty on dozens of occasions. Roland had no doubt that Pete would rush to Roland's aid if the meeting with the Axis agents went south. Roland also had every intention of double-crossing Pete if the Axis agents insisted that only one could escape with them to safety.

Roland turned back to the sea, knowing that somehow his contact must come from the cliffs. *How?* Roland asked himself. *How is he going to . . . ?* Roland's thoughts were cut short as he became aware of a numbness spreading across his body.

The numbness crept into Roland's fingers and toes. The traitor tried to flex his fingers to chase the numbness away. Roland realized, *My fingers. They aren't moving.*

Fear flooded into Roland as he tried to flex his arms, his legs, or even to take a step. Roland realized that his ability to move was being drained away, as was his ability to think. His thoughts were starting to break into small fragments, as if he was fighting to stay awake and failing.

He became aware of a humming. Roland could hear and feel the humming—the humming that sounded and felt like thousands of bees in the air, all so close they caused Roland's entire body to vibrate.

Roland's eyes were locked on the very edge of the cliffs of Weymouth. At the edge of the cliff, in the dim moonlight, Roland saw it.

An impossibly long and thin arm was at the edge of the cliff, appearing over the cliff's side. Roland somehow forced the thought to his mind, *What is that? A huge bug? A baby doe-sized spider?* Even in his paralyzed state, Roland couldn't believe his eyes, couldn't accept that the strange limb belonged to a man. No man could be on the face of the cliff, hundreds of feet above the water.

The limb stretched from the cliff-edge and reached for solid ground on the edge of the Weymouth field. Impossibly long fingers flexed and grabbed at the ground. Made strong by dark magick, the fingers burrowed into the dirt.

A second long, thin arm swung in the air. The second arm mirrored the actions of the first, reaching ground, its long thin fingers flexing and then grabbing purchase. The creature then worked at getting itself from the cliff-face to the Weymouth field.

The man-spider thing kept its torso close to the ground, its chest hugging the vertical side of the cliff. When the creature's head appeared over the edge, the creature pushed its face into the dirt of the Weymouth field. The arms dragged the creature's torso up. As the creature's pelvis cleared the edge of the cliff, it pivoted its body, so the man-creature's torso was parallel to the ground. The creature then hugged the ground with its chest and burrowed a track in the dirt as it moved forward, keeping its upper arms and elbows pointed up.

The creature's legs were barely thicker than thin baby saplings and seemed to have hips joints that were put in backwards. As it scuttled forward, its thighs were straight up in the air, like a Sparassidae spider. At the knees, the creature's legs bent to the ground. The knees appeared to swing at an angle that moved laterally, and its lower legs ended in near stumps, its feet having curled and rotted in small knobs.

The creature moved in a spider-type way, pulling with its arms as well as push-crawling with its feet. Its face was in the dirt, with only its eyes showing.

The eyes were where the power of the creature resided. The thin arms and bony legs of the thing that scuttled in the dirt looked as if they could be broken by a sharp movement, but the eyes of the creature broadcast power.

Those eyes locked on Roland. Roland willed himself

to think, *Run,* but his body didn't obey the running command. The creature started to scuttle towards Roland impossibly fast.

Roland could feel himself start to sweat in fear. He tried harder to run, and he commanded himself, *Move! Move into the safety of the trees!*

His body started to shake. A wave of nausea rolled through him as he realized his body was starting to walk towards the creature.

Oh no. Oh God, no, Roland prayed.

Roland heard the shotgun blast from a tent, yards from where he hid. The creature screeched a cry that was a cross behind a wounded animal and person. It leaped at least fifteen feet in the air and landed steps from the edge of the cliff, facing towards the sea.

British agents rushed from a smattering of tents and tried to catch the creature before it disappeared over the edge of the cliff. But they didn't have a chance. Even wounded, the fast-moving creature had too much of a lead.

The British special-agents reached the edge of the cliff. A civilian, hidden in one of the dozens of tents, called to them.

"Can you see it?"

An agent called back, "I'm afraid not, Mr. Crowley."

The entire scene began to make sense to Roland. Aleister Crowley was the famed British occultist. Somewhere, somehow, British intelligence had learned the Axis were desperate enough to engage in occult warfare. The British had employed their own spell-casters to counter the threat. Crowley had either used divination to predict the creature, or a captured Axis spy had given the occult creature up in exchange for leniency.

Roland watched Crowley hurry towards the Weymouth Forest. As Crowley approached the trees, Roland saw a series of squiggly lines and circles poking out from under the collar of the spell-caster. Roland guessed the lines were some type of counter-magick to combat the power of the creature. Crowley commanded the special agents, "Check the edge of the forest. It seemed to be heading towards the trees."

Roland realized he could move again and ran as deep into the forest as he could.

Running through the forest, Roland heard Mr. Crowley tell the soldiers that had been woken up by the shotgun blast, "Everyone, back to your tents. Nothing to see here. Get ready for the big day tomorrow." Roland also heard Pete Kolems start to protest his innocence to the British agents, "No, you don't understand. I am just out for a walk!"

Roland made it back to his tent without being discovered. Crawling into his sleeping bag, he prepared a lie to tell any MPs who might have discovered his night's activities. Roland decided the classic, "I don't know what you are talking about; I never left the tent all night; Petey is a liar!" was his best option.

Still worried about the morning's possible battle, Roland took a barbiturate pill from his small stash of stolen sleep-aids. As Roland fell asleep, his last thought was, *How am I going to make my money back from this stupid talisman?*

CHAPTER 4

On July 12, 1944, August Ording fled Britain at midnight in a Heinkel He 51 biplane, an aircraft that was essentially a large kite with an engine. The biplane, ancient even by World War II aviation standards, had been riddled with bullets by the anti-aircraft guns of a British Coastal Battery fortification.

August heard the engine of his plane, a modified motorcycle engine, cough. Trying to fight the panic that washed through him, August wondered if the English mechanic who took German money felt bad about betraying his country. August didn't think so, as the mechanic's accent had just a touch of Irish.

August Ording's thoughts stopped when he heard

the plane engine give a final loud cough and then die. He watched the plane's propeller stop rotating. The occultist realized he would be able to glide a few hundred yards, so August aimed his plane towards the beach in the distance and repeated the mantra, "Just have to touch down in France, and I am safe. Just have to touch down in France, and I am safe!"

August glided over the barbed-wired protected sand, looking for a landmark that would tell him exactly what French beach he would be landing on. *Biarritz? Nice? Saint-Tropez?* August could barely see the fox-holes inside the wired perimeter. The defense dug-outs were stuffed with three soldiers each and the outline of Schneider 75 machine guns.

It took August Ording a full minute to realize what he had seen, and another minute before the thought formed in his head. *Schneider 75? Those aren't French guns! Those are Spanish!*

August glanced into the night sky, praying and hoping that the position of the moon and stars would tell him something different from what his eyes were seeing. The stars, which August should have watched and not the shot-to-pieces compass and rotating plotter in the flimsy dashboard, confirmed what August already knew. He was way off course.

Ording glanced down at the ground and realized he

was only feet above land. There was no way he could fly any farther. He banked his plane so he would glide onto the sand of the beach.

Ording glanced around him. The Spanish military forces he had glided over had sent soldiers to intercept and detain him. *The only reason the Spaniards didn't shoot me down was because I am a single old plane. If I am caught, the Spaniards will interrogate me.*

Fear ran through Ording as he remembered soldier's stories about the brutality of the Dictator of Spain's interrogations.

Ording wasn't a ranger or commando, the type of soldier that could survive a chase in the Spanish country-side. Ording was an occultist, but he wasn't a shaman or witch that could thrive in the wilderness. Ording was a librarian before the war; his army training had built on his research skills. The army had tasked Ording with finding some type of obscure occult system that could help the war effort.

Before his missions, August Ording had spent his time learning runes, hieroglyphics, sacred geometric symbols, as well as the chants needed to activate the power of mystical writing. Armed with his knowledge, Ording had chased money and glory and power. Ording had promised the Axis command that he had found an occult super-weapon, which he would be happy to recreate for the glory of the Empire.

Ording's superiors were delighted at the news. The commanders gave August Ording a promotion, a bump in pay, and a personal servant.

After all of the Axis command had gotten the hieroglyph tattoos that would protect them from Ording's creature, the Axis high command gave Ording a platoon of recruits to turn into an occult war machine.

Ording's magick had failed on the soldiers. One had died from the magick rituals, the others had lost their minds. Only one soldier survived Ording's tattooing and fasting process, but the process had destroyed man mentally and physically. August's disappointed superiors snidely called August Ording's creature the "*die schädel.*" Ording obstinately swore the creature would be a viable occult weapon.

Ording and the creature failed on its first mission. As punishment, the Axis command took away Ording's personal servant.

After the creature's second failure, Ording's superiors knocked him down a rank and cut his pay.

After his third failure, as he fled back home to the Empire, Ording knew he would have much to explain to his superiors.

Landing the crippled plane, Ording realized the gravity of his situation and thought, *I will deal with my commanders if I ever get back to the Axis Empire. Right now, I must plan for Spain.*

The Caudillo of Spain kept his country neutral, but is paranoia over occult warfare. The dictator's policy is to have occultists executed on sight.

Ording's crippled plane bounced on the ground and rolled to a halt on the sand of the beach. Troops surrounded his plane, arriving by jeep.

The Caudillo Francisco Franco maintains control of Spain with a mix of authoritarianism, nationalism, and Catholicism.

Catholicism, realized Ording. *That's the key. I must wrap myself in Catholicism. Be a priest and survive.*

Sitting in his plane, Ording saw the detachment of Franco's Army dismount from their jeeps feet from him. A dozen yards past him on the interior side of the Spanish beach, past the gun fortifications, walked a family: a man, a woman, and a young boy.

The occultist knew the Francoist Army didn't believe in coincidence, and the random couple on the beach would have trouble saving themselves. *Franco's Army may let the woman go, but the man? Never!*

Pushing the thoughts of the couple out of his mind, Ording muttered one of the few spells he knew that could help his situation. It was a simple spell of enchantment, a spell that makes fools believe lies. After he finished muttering the spell, Ording prayed that the Sergeant who walked towards him was a fool. Then Ording got out of the plane with his hands raised.

In Ording's occult studies, he had become an expert in Latin, the language of the Catholic Church. As Ording muttered the prayers of the Church as loud as he could, he saw the soldiers lower their guns. The occultist allowed himself to think, *I may get out of this yet.*

On the beach, Ording heard the woman cry in Spanish, "No, No, NO! My name is Roxanne, and we know nothing about that man in the plane!"

CHAPTER 5

BERHTRAM BRAUN HAD A CIGARETTE HANGING FROM HIS mouth and the exhausted look of a man who had fought for years to escape some type of prison and failed. The former Axis private and Army deserter begged Mr. Brett, "I can't live in the desert anymore. Help me get to America."

It was 1952 in Madrid, Spain, in the windowless interrogation offices of Spain's Social Investigation Brigade. S.I.B. special agent Mr. Brett sat across from the sunburnt ex-soldier, the wild man who wouldn't let go of his leather bag. Mr. Brett realized, *This man is half-mad from his wanderings, but even crazy men sometimes know real secrets.*

In heavily accented Spanish, holding his cigarette between his fingers as he spoke, Berhtram pleaded, "I was just a farm boy when the Axis conscripted me into the war. I know nothing."

Mr. Brett asked, "If you know nothing, you are no help to me."

A stunned Berhtram sat in silence.

Mr. Brett restarted the conversation. "How did you get to Ceuta?"

Ceuta was an autonomous city of Spain on the North African coast, surrounded by the Kingdom of Morocco.

Berhtram answered, "In the war, I was assigned to the occult warfare division. I was the personal assistant of August Ording."

Mr. Brett flatly stated, "I have never heard of this person."

Berhtram pleaded, "You must have. In Alamein, it was Ording who led the *die schädel* into the bunkers, to murder the soldiers. It is a creature over six feet tall, capable of controlling a soldier's mind."

Excitement shot through Mr. Brett, but he let no emotion show. The S.I.B. agent knew of the *die schädel* from intelligence collected and shared by the British Army. Mr. Brett had always been eager for more information on the mind-controlling creature, as such information was the only thing capable of impressing Dictator Franco.

With no emotion, Mr. Brett asked, "How do you know this thing?"

Berhtram said, "Because I was there." The pleading returned to Berhtram's voice as he added, "I had to be. I was a soldier. I was ordered to be August Ording's personal assistant. To carry his water into battle! But at the first chance, I ran."

Mr. Brett asked, "You ran? During the battle, into the desert?"

"Yes!" Berhtram said. "When Ording had his back turned, when the bombs were raining down, I took a chance. I ran. Into the Egyptian desert."

Mr. Brett stated, "The chances of survival in the Alamein Desert are almost zero."

Berhtram crossed his arms as he said, "That's right. My chance at survival was almost zero. That's why the Axis never looked for me. They assumed if the bombs didn't kill me, the Allies would. And if the Allies didn't kill me, the desert would. But I survived all three dangers."

"Congratulations. But your ability to survive doesn't explain why you are here, or why I should help you."

Berhtram continued, "I couldn't go back home after the war. Who knows how many Axis loyalists were waiting in the years after the war ended, hoping that the Axis surrender was temporary? How many fanatics hid in the shadows waiting to kill a conscript who quit fighting?"

"So, after the war, you stayed in Africa?" Mr. Brett asked.

Berhtram nodded. "I worked my way across Egypt,

through Morocco."

Mr. Brett prompted, "Now you want out of the desert?"

Berhtram answered, "Now I want a new life in America. California! The beach, surfing. Bikinis. As former Axis, I doubt American officials would let me in. But Spain! The S.I.B. has a reputation for giving new identities to someone with something to trade. With a new I.D., I could make it to the sunshine state." Berhtram smiled as he continued, "The Axis high command would never let Ording develop an occult weapon without some personal protection for themselves. I could tell you the grimoire that contains the hieroglyphs that offer personal protection from the powers of the *die schädel*. Your Caudillo Franco would like such information."

Mr. Brett considered this. "We already have the information. British intelligence gave us a copy of the hieroglyphs years ago. There was no appreciation by President Franco. He would rather be burned at the stake as a heretic than be tattooed with some heathen symbol."

A crestfallen look appeared on Berhtram's face. The ex-soldier started to stutter, "This is how August controls the *die schädel*. August binds the creature's spirit to a mirror. A magick mirror."

Mr. Brett called to the S.I.B. agents waiting in the hall outside of the interrogation room, "Guards!" When the guards entered, Mr. Brett pointed at Berhtram. "Throw this man on a steamship back to Morocco. He is of no use to me."

Berhtram started to stutter as he backed away from the guards. "The mirror! Control of the mirror—"

Mr. Brett interrupted, "We know all about how the creature is bound to the spell-caster using a magick mirror, again thanks to Mr. Crowley of British intelligence. You are really not very helpful."

Backed into a corner, Berhtram squealed, "Do you know where Ording is? The *Paishiyauvada* Amulet of Illusion Removal could help in locating him!"

Mr. Brett raised his hands, indicating the guards to stop. Berhtram opened the bag he carried and pulled out a bronze medal. "The closer this amulet is to Ording, the weaker the spells that keep him hidden will become. I'm guessing Ording is in Madrid. If you let me stay, I will make it my prime duty to use this amulet to unmask my former Sergeant."

Mr. Brett considered this new information. "How do I know this works?"

Berhtram answered, "You have to take the chance that it does. The occult war isn't over."

Sensing the sincerity in Berhtram's voice, Mr. Brett asked, "What do you mean?"

Berhtram responded, "The insane leaders of the Axis powers planned for defeat. When the Axis Empire fell, Axis loyalists were instructed to wait seven years. To take seven years to blend into society. At the end of the seventh year, the loyalists would re-start the war. But the re-ignited war would be a war without clear-cut soldiers. It would be a war that struck from shadows. A terror war." Berhtram played with the medallion in his fingers as he continued. "Have the British told you about the amulet of *Jomhuri-ye Eslâmi-ye?* The amulet stolen from the British museum? The amulet that can increase the power of the *die schädel* by one-thousand percent? Would your President-For-Life allow himself to be tattooed if there was the possibility that his personal bodyguard's minds could be taken over at any minute? From anywhere?"

Berhtram finished with what he knew would clinch the deal. "Do you know what Ording looks like? I do."

Mr. Brett waved the guards away and said to Berhtram, "Let's make a deal."

CHAPTER 6

AUGUST ORDING, THE FUGITIVE OCCULTIST, LISTENED TO the pounding on his dorm-room door and thought, *The bastards have found me out.*

It was 1952 in Madrid, Spain. August was in his dorm in Las Descalzas Reales Monastery, a former palace for the Royal Family of Spain. In 1945, President-For-Life Franco seized and donated the Las Descalzas Reales to the Catholic Church with the condition the building be used for housing clergy.

Dictator Franco had an ulterior motive for helping members of the cloth. Franco was terrified of the Axis war machine's sorcery and believed keeping as many practicing priests in the heart of Madrid, steps from the

Presidential Palace, would protect him from the dark magick spell casters of the Axis.

After arriving in Spain, Ording assumed a new persona as a priest. At first, August Ording's new life in Spain had worked out wonderfully for the occultist. During the day, the spell-weaver used an influence spell to convince the state and church bureaucracy that he was an innocent Catholic Priest. At night, to make money for retirement in America, Ording sold spells and charms to thrill-seekers in the Madrid criminal world.

But things had collapsed for Ording in the past hours. Bishop deFranco, the deeply religious authority who ran the monastery, had started to notice things about Ording— Ording's absence at Vespers, Ording's shallow knowledge of prayers and sacraments—that the occultist's spells had always kept hidden. The spells were weakening.

Bishop deFranco pounded on Ording's door and called, "Brother August? We need to talk about your devotion. I am concerned your heart is not where it should be."

Ording called back, "Can we talk tomorrow, Father? I feel ill."

Ording could feel the indecision radiating from Bishop deFranco, but the senior holy man ultimately called to Ording, "Of course. Feel better."

Ording breathed a sigh of relief when he heard deFranco shuffle away.

The reality hit Ording hard. *My influence and camou-flage spells are losing their power,* Ording admitted to himself, and briefly wondered why. *Perhaps the British occultists were launching a new mystic attack? Perhaps Franco's mystics were chanting harder?* Ultimately, Ording just accepted his reality and started to plan an escape from his adopted life.

The smell of the monastery's barnyard and stable, separated from the monastery by a thin alley, reached Ording's nostrils. He would not miss the monastery.

Even the view from Ording's third-floor room caused him irritation. The room was in the back of the palace, facing the stables he hated, hidden from sunlight and the streets of Spain.

Ording pushed his feelings of self-pity aside and thought, *If the camouflage spells are failing, I do not dare cross at a legitimate port. The risk of Franco's anti-occult S.I.B. Agents is too great. I'll need to be smuggled to America.*

But the only people who could smuggle him to California was the Apache Crime Family, and help from the Apaches cost money.

Ording sat upright, opened the drawer on the nightstand next to his bed, and looked at his magick mirror. Ording had constructed the simple magick tool days earlier, when the illusions spells started to fade in power.

The die schädel failed as a weapon of war, but in service

to the Apaches, it will get me out of Spain!

Ording took a cigarette butt, picture frame, black paint and brush, drawing paper, and a pencil from the night-stand.

I shall create a new die schädel. It will get me out of Spain. I'll get revenge on the bastard that caused me to be trapped here, and I'll start the new war!

Ording had drawn a very rough picture of Thadeus Martin on the drawing paper. Ording reviewed the poor drawing, and hoped that his limited ability would be enough to make the magick work. He removed the glass from the picture frame and placed the picture on the glass, so he could see his drawing through the glass, and then flipped the glass and picture over. The back of the picture faced Ording and lay on top of the glass.

Ording started to paint one side of the glass black, with the sticky paint covering the drawing paper, the paint seeping through the paper. Ording lay the painted glass on the floor, with the painted side facing him, the paint gluing the paper to the glass, the drawing facing the glass. He let the paint dry for a few minutes, and then started to trace commonplace geometric figures in the paint. The shapes Ording drew in the paint had been discovered by the Greek sorcerer Pythagoras. The majority of humanity had forgotten the shapes were sacred and powerful.

The first figure Ording traced was the circle—the sacred geometry symbol of wholeness. Centuries earlier, practitioners of the occult arts discovered that by meditating on a circle, the human mind could link to any other mind in the universe, as every mind is part of the wholeness of all that is.

Ording then traced a triangle on the perimeter of the circle, on the part of the circle that faced closest to North. The triangle was the hermetic symbol that symbolized harmony to the subconsciousness mind.

As he drew, Ording thought, *Connect to one, connect to all.*

At the southernmost part of the circle, Ording drew an inverted triangle.

Connect to one, disconnect the one from all.

At the easternmost part of the circle, Ording drew a cross.

Connect to one, connect to all.

At the western most part of the circle, Ording drew a square, the symbol that symbolized isolation.

Connect to one, disconnect the one from all.

Inside the circle, Ording drew a sigil—a series of wavy lines. To the untrained eye, the squiggles looked like random scratches a child would make. But the occultist knew better.

A demon-sigil was a mark that allowed a skilled occultist to call a demon. For centuries, the general public assumed demon-sigils were useless scratches put on cave walls by ignorant peoples. The Axis occultist knew different.

Demons were called using a variety of senses. Ording knew the sense of sight—seeing the sigil—was just one key used to open the portal the demon would use to enter Earth.

Ording hissed a call to the demon Dècaraia, the Genii of hate for the dead Mohenjo-Daro tribe. "Hear me, Dècaraia, and bring destruction to that boy that led to my imprisonment."

Out of all the people Ording hated, Ording hated Thadeus the most. Ording hated the humiliation he felt, he hated the way the young boy had cried out during his mission in London, and he hated that what should have been his biggest triumph was nothing. Over the years, Ording had cursed Thadeus multiple times, and every night Ording prayed to the left-hand path Gods of forgotten civilizations that Thadeus would suffer.

Ording hissed, "Great Dècaraia, bring that boy, that insolent bastard, to me! Allow me to make him into a new, better *die schädel*—a creature that will free me from this prison!"

The smell of tobacco overwhelmed Ording. *Tobacco? What does this mean?*

The tobacco smell vanished, replaced by the taste of blood in Ording's mouth, overwhelming him, and a huge smile burst onto his face. *Revenge,* thought Ording, *Revenge is on its way. The start of the new war is coming.*

CHAPTER 7

Mr. Brett, a special agent for Spain's intelligence network, stood on the Atocha train platform determined to get more intelligence about the latest terror threat to his country.

It was 1952 in Madrid. As Jacques Proust deboarded the Paris-Madrid express at the Puerta de Atocha station onto the crowded train platform, someone clamped hard on his right arm.

Pain shot up Jacques' arm, from the elbow to the shoulder. The war vet turned to demand an explanation and apology from the groper, but was stunned to hear a very ordinary man whisper, "Do you have a moment, sir?"

As Jacques looked into the expressionless face of the

man on his right, he felt the tough, solid body of another man on his left, delivering the warning, *Don't run.*

Jacques glanced at the other passengers on the train platform. The crowd that poured out of the train were exhausted after the nine-hour trek from France. As the throng grabbed luggage, looked for a porter, or tried to spot a lost family member, Jacques realized as long as Franco's men kept their voices down, no one would realize that Franco's Social Investigation Brigade was even on the platform.

The members of Franco's police were tough, intelligent, and had been trained not only in discretion but in the martial arts of Bartitsu and Schwingen. *Running would be a very bad idea,* realized Jacques. *They'll catch and beat me before I get ten feet. When I am unconscious, they'll show some badges to the crowd, claim they are metro police, that I am a pickpocket and drag me away.*

Jacques heard the officer on his right say, "Nothing bad, sir. You're not in any trouble. We just need your help in clearing up a few things."

Jacques knew the men would say the same thing even if he was hip-deep in trouble.

I haven't done anything, Jacques told himself.

Jacques told the officers, "Certainly, always happy to help."

The officers introduced themselves as Mr. Brett and Mr. Charles. With Mr. Brett in front and Mr. Charles behind,

Jacques was led to the out-of-sight police station hidden in the depths of the train terminal. As the trio walked off the platform and into the building of the station, the army vet pondered how much evidence the officers had against him.

Nothing. They have nothing, Jacques Proust guessed. But, knowing the severe penalties for practicing witchcraft in the obsessed dictator's country, Jacques couldn't help but ask himself, *Unless I screwed up somewhere?*

Ever since Jacques' brush with the sorcery in World War II, he'd become more and more obsessed with the occult. His once-a-year trip to Britain to visit Stonehenge had grown into weekly train trips to France's Bibliothèque Nationale de France, which had the most extensive collection of occult writings in the western hemisphere. The writings of Hermes Trismegistus, essays on mystic practices of the East, tracks on Yogic and Shamanism practices were all found on the dusty shelves of the library.

Franco's men caught on, thought Jacques. *Someone, somewhere, squealed on me and told the S.I.B. how I have been spending my weekends.*

But who? Jacques hadn't mentioned his obsession with anyone. He pushed suspicions on who betrayed him aside and contemplated his legal defense. *So what if someone squealed that I spend my weekends in France? There are dozens of other American expats who work in Madrid and have a slice of honey on the side in France! Going to Paris doesn't mean I practice magick!*

Jacques knew he could explain the trips to Paris, but he couldn't explain away the binder stuffed with notes on occultism back at his apartment, which contained pages of scribblings and notes on how modern religious habits were the vestiges of occult practices, how the Sign of the Cross was developed to be used during exorcisms, how magick had its roots in mysticism, how the Old Testament talked of sorcerers and spell-casters.

So what if they found my notebook? Jacques told himself. *Is it illegal to keep a diary? Make some notes about trivia?* Jacques forced himself to believe his lie, convinced himself that the baloney he told himself was a believable defense to Franco's men.

After a series of twists and turns in a length of gray hallways, Jacques and the officers reached a door like any other. He held his breath, knowing that when the door was flung open, whatever was inside would tell him how long he had to live.

After the war, Jacques had heard horrifying tales where the desperate communist leadership of the Soviet Union kidnapped Russians citizens from the streets of Moscow. Inside tile-lined rooms, the Russian secret police would strip the Russian naked and begin a beating until the civilian either died or provided information on a neighbor or relative who was anti-communist. Since the rooms were lined with tiles, the victim's blood could be easily washed down the drain.

Jacques saw no reason why Franco's squad wouldn't use the same methods to get what they wanted. *Instead of an anti-communist, they want me to name an occultist. If the room inside has nothing but a drain and tiles, I am a dead man.*

Franco's men popped open the door and Jacques saw a room with a desk, chairs, and a linoleum floor. Jacques breathed a sigh of relief. Then Mr. Brett spoke.

"We found some very interesting things today, Mr. Proust!" the officer said as he pulled Jacques' notebook from a drawer in the desk and sat down. Jacques felt the solidness drain from his legs. He could feel himself reeling, going light-headed. The thought *No, no, no* started to pound into his brain.

He was on the verge of fainting when he heard, "Would you like some coffee, Mr. Proust?"

Jacques was confused at the words. A part of him asked, *Why are we talking about coffee? My life could be coming to an end? Why are we talking about coffee?*

Jacques heard the question again, "Would you like some coffee, Mr. Proust? Or maybe you would like to sit down?" The banality of the officer's questions forced the idea into Jacques' mind. *I'm not in trouble. They don't care about my notebook. No one could be asking me about coffee and to sit down if they cared about my notebook.*

Jacques stuttered, "Coffee. Coffee would be fine."

Mr. Charles gently steered him to the chair, helping him sit down. As Jacques sat still for a few minutes, Mr. Charles produced two cups of coffee, one for Mr. Brett and one for Jacques.

Mr. Brett silently sipped his coffee and Jacques did the same. As the two drank, Jacques' denial of his situation faded from his brain. He saw his binder, full of notes on various magick rituals, sitting on the desk in front of Mr. Brett.

Why haven't they thrown me in jail? Jacques asked himself. *Why am I here?*

Mr. Brett put his coffee down and smiled. From his time in military service, Jacques knew that whenever a man behind a desk smiled, it was because the man in front of the desk was in a very compromising position.

Mr. Brett said, "Jacques, you are an American? Yes? But your mother is French. That is why you move around in Paris so well."

Jacques nodded.

Mr. Brett continued, "I have a little bit of a problem, and I need a unique man to help solve it. You are a unique man."

Jacques realized, *He needs information. He needs information about something.*

"As you know, Jacques, any practice of the occult in

Spain is a capital offense. What you may not know is that whenever something is illegal, the illegality of the product makes it desirable to the weak-minded and corrupt."

Jacques nodded, indicating he understood but did not necessarily agree with the position.

"Those French gilipollas masquerading as gangsters, the Apaches, have made a small business importing occult artifacts to sell to our good Spanish youth," Mr. Brett said.

Realization started to come together in Jacques' mind.

Mr. Brett's hand slid across the desk and lightly tapped Jacques' notebook. "You know something about the occult, Jacques. These scribbles, they are not a serious crime and will be forgotten when you are back in America. But first we really do need your help in a matter."

Everything gelled and made sense to Jacques. *If I help them out, they will forget my crime and let me run to the U.S. when I am done.*

"You will help us out, won't you, Jacques?"

Jacques had a few run-ins with the Apaches during his trips to Paris, and knew the members of the Apache gang were pimps, pickpockets, thieves, and loan sharks. Jacques said, "Sure. I have no love for those lowlifes."

"Excellent," Mr. Brett remarked. "If you could start working the crowd in a bar called Micheal's that would be great."

Jacques nodded that he understood.

"Excellent," Mr. Brett repeated.

As he got up to leave, Jacques asked, "How did you find out about my trips?"

Mr. Brett ignored the question and said, "Stop by Micheal's; get your bearings. I'll call you later."

CHAPTER 8

Roland O'Brien stared nervously at the three men across from him. He knew if he judged incorrectly, the men would have him reported to the Dictator of Spain's Brigada de Investigación Social. *The S.I.B.*, Roland realized, *would throw me in a prison cell so deep and dark I would never see the light of day again.*

It was 1952 in Madrid. Roland swallowed hard, steeled his nerves, and thought, *There is so much money on the line, it's a chance I have to take. I've told too many lies since 1945 to chicken out now.*

At the end of the war in 1945, Private Zack Smithburg offered fellow Private Roland O'Brien a job in the newly formed Madrid-based Smithburg Office Supply

Corporation. The company was successful, grew rapidly, and made millions of pesetas in profit. Of those millions, Mr. O'Brien stole thousands from Smithburg via forgery and fraud. By 1952, Zack Smithburg had started to suspect that his good friend Roland was dipping his hand into the company cookie jar.

At first, Zack dropped barely disguised hints to his long-time business associate that the excessive spending and excessive cash draws should stop, saying, "Business is good, but we don't seem to be making as much profit as I thought," and "Maybe the company should cut down on spending. What do you think, Roland?"

For the first weeks when Zack dropped his hints, Roland would reply, "Of course! Times aren't what they used to be!"

Zack hoped these changes would happen because by 1952, the Caudillo of Spain had started to enforce extreme morality laws. Even the hint of immorality, such as Roland's suspected affairs with various women, could bring a visit from Spain's morality police. The S.I.B. had the authority to send adulterers, heretics, and blasphemers to prison, seize the money, and confiscate assets.

Roland's spending didn't stop. Cash draws were still happening, Smithburg Office Supply was still getting bills from accounts for which bookkeepers could find no records, rumors of illicit affairs still circulated among the

Smithburg staff.

Zack started to get notes from the Smithburg legal staff. The awkwardly worded hypothetical scenarios indicated that if an employee was found guilty of Spain's anti-morality laws, then the company he worked for could be found liable. Zack Smithburg hired Stacy Gomez, a no-nonsense certified accountant, as Smithburg Office Supplies new General Treasurer. Roland O'Brien nearly fainted with relief when he heard a woman had been hired to dig-up his misdeeds. Roland considered himself Casanova reborn and believed romancing an accountant to do his bidding would be easy.

On Ms. Gomez's first day, Roland walked into her office, closed the door, and said he would like to get to know her better. Ms. Gomez asked Roland to open the office door and suggested they could talk over coffee in the always-crowded Smithburg cafeteria. Roland turned around and stomped out of Ms. Gomez's office.

On Ms. Gomez's second day, Roland walked into her office, closed the door, and told Ms. Gomez that she had the most beautiful eyes he had ever seen. Ms. Gomez pressed the intercom on her desk and asked her admin assistant to come in.

Asking an admin assistant to come into an office was standard practice in Franco's Spain, although usually done by men. Men had taken to having witnesses to all interactions with ladies in the office to avoid any talk that could get them in trouble with the Dictator's morality police. When Ms. Gomez's assistant walked in, Roland walked out.

Waking up the third morning of Ms. Gomez's employment, Roland knew the no-nonsense accountant would soon have enough evidence against him to get him fired. For the first time, Roland realized how much money he had 'borrowed' from the company.

Roland came up with a huge lie to escape justice. On the fourth day of Ms. Gomez's employment, Roland convinced himself that the lie would work and went to the Smithburg offices.

At the Smithburg building, Roland walked into the Smithburg's Human Resources office, closed the door behind him, and whispered to the head of Human Resources, "Stacy Gomez had a man in her office last night."

The mouth of Mrs. Gloria Sanchez, the Head of Human Resources, dropped open in shock. Only Roland's calming lie, told in monotone, prevented Mrs. Sanchez from fainting.

"I was coming home from dinner with friends and remembered I left my Bible in my office. I always like to end the day by reading Psalms . . ." lied Roland, ". . . so I thought I would swing by the office and pick up my things . . ." Roland stopped talking when he saw the flailing hands and red-embarrassed face of Mrs. Sanchez, begging him to stop talking. Mrs. Sanchez was terrified of the Brigada de Investigación Social.

As Mrs. Sanchez waved her arms at Roland and told him to get out of her office, she muttered, "Don't, don't, don't speak anymore. I'll . . . I'll . . ."

Roland took Mrs. Sanchez's actions and muttering to mean, "I'll take care of Stacy Gomez. Just don't tell anyone about the sex!"

Stacy Gomez was transferred to the copy-assistant division, three pay-grades lower than General Treasurer. She quit in disgust. Roland marched into Zack's office and demanded to know how Zack could have used such poor judgment, asking, "Don't you know what would happen if we get caught promoting some floozy? Where do you think we are, Las Vegas?"

As Roland attempted to brow-beat the company CEO, Roland saw something he hadn't seen in Zack Smithburg before. Roland saw hate well up in the eyes of his boss.

Glaring at Roland, Zack growled, "Thanks for letting me know about Ms. Gomez. I'll see to it that the situation is corrected."

As Roland left Zack's office, the thief and liar realized he had gone too far.

Chapter 9

Jacques Proust became a top-notch informant for Spain's Social Investigation Brigade.

It was 1952 in Madrid. Magick practitioners, hated by the paranoid Dictator Francesco Franco, were hunted by Spain's government. Proust's recruitment to the bureau that exterminated people unnecessary to Spain turned out to be a wonderful move for both the S.I.B. and the French-American.

Jacques Proust's method for discovering victims was as effective as dragging a fishing net through a salmon-ladened stream. Proust haunted a bar called Micheal's. Proust showed up every evening, sat on a bar stool, and trolled for victims.

Jacques' victims fell into two categories. The first type of victim were young men and women who had just moved to Madrid from the country and were out spending their first big paycheck. Jacques had snared a dozen half-drunk adventure seekers by promising them something unusual, something exciting. Jacques took the naïve youngsters to a seance. On Jacques' signal, S.I.B. agents raided the seance. Under threat of prison, the youngsters agreed to become informants.

The second type of victim, and the type that was more lucrative to Jacques, were men whose lifetime of poor decisions had caught up to them. Jacques victimized gamblers, habitual cannabis users, drunkards, and womanizers who had messed up their lives and were desperate for a quick fix to their problems. Jacques would work his way into a conversation with the desperate man and brag.

Jacques would brag about knowing about a crime, about how a friend of a friend had pulled off a scam, about how a friend of a friend had scammed his employer out of a dozen pesetas with some simple paperwork trick. At the beginning of his relationship with a broken man, Jacques never claimed he was a criminal. Jacques just dropped hints that he knew someone that committed a successful crime. Depending on how the broken man reacted, Jacques knew whether to continue the scam or not. If the man smiled, Jacques knew to pursue the relationship. If the man frowned and left the bar, Jacques knew to fish elsewhere.

Jacques had been working on Roland O'Brien for a week and a half. In their first drinking session, Jacques successfully slipped an anecdote about a friend of a friend stealing cars before Roland's third and fourth shots of Jameson. Jacques saw a smile spread on Roland's face.

In his second conversation with Roland, Jacques humble-bragged about a friend of a friend that had stolen hundreds through fraud. In his third conversation with Roland, Jacques told a funny story of extortion, of a friend of a friend that made a bunch of money claiming he found an occult artifact in a neighbor's yard. Jacques remembered clapping Roland on the back and exclaiming, "The old man was so scared, he paid my buddy half a dozen pesetas just to get rid of the thing!"

Roland's eyes opened in disbelief that a dictator could instill such fear into a population about something as unbelievable as witchcraft. Still Jacques knew, *Someday, Roland is going to ask me about the occult scam.*

ON THE EVENING OF THE DAY WHERE ROLAND HAD LIED about Stacy Gomez, Jacques walked into Micheal's bar, saw Roland, read Roland's body language, and thought, *Roland O'Brien, you big beautiful fat fish, tonight is the night I finally reel you in.*

Jacques clapped Roland on the back, gave a cheery, "Hello, Roland!" ordered a pint, and sat on the bar-stool next to Roland. Jacques hid his smile when Roland pushed closed and whispered, "Hey, you remembered that thing you told me? About the occult stuff?"

Jacques screwed up his face in confusion, pretending not to know what Roland was talking about. After a half-second, Jacques forced a look of comprehension to his face and muttered, "A-Ha! The occult gag." Knowing any further games weren't necessary, Jacques asked, "Who is the victim?"

Roland whispered, "Zack Smithburg. He owns Smithburg Office Supplies."

Jacques couldn't hide his surprise when realization set in that Roland wanted to con a very successful man out of hundreds of pesetas. Surprise was quickly replaced with fear.

"Roland," Jacques began, "The occult scam is something run on pensioners and old ladies. Paint a box with some red pentagrams, bury it in a yard, have some kids dig it up and tell the owner of the house the authorities won't like a Satan-box being found. The retired bastard gives a few coins to get rid of the thing."

"Running a scam on someone like Zack Smithburg is different. A guy like Zack won't panic. A guy like Zack might call the police, attempt to get to the bottom of the situation. For a few pesetas, it's better to find a victim with less confidence and fewer resources."

Roland grunted at Jacques. "You got it all wrong. I don't want to extort the bastard. I want the bastard to get disappeared by the S.I.B."

There was a second of confusion as Jacques tried to understand Roland's plan, but then Jacques' brain started to follow Roland's thinking.

Jacques muttered, "Zack has something you want, something more than just some random cash."

Roland muttered, "I'm second in command at Smithburg Office Supplies. With Zack gone, I can run the place the way it should be run. Make some real money."

Jacques nodded in understanding, and thought, *Roland, you lying two-faced son of a bitch. Zack has something on you. Did you get Zack's daughter pregnant? Or maybe Zack caught you with your hand in the cookie jar? No one had ever wanted their boss to fall into the hands of Franco's jailers because they thought a business should be run differently.*

Jacques quickly did the math, considering Roland's proposal, thinking how many lies he would have to tell, thinking how much cash he could grab before Franco's S.I.B. would figure out the scam. The big thought in Jacques' head was, *I can make enough cash from this to get smuggled out of Spain, and then I'll dump Roland off with Mr. Brett and ditch the S.I.B.*

Jacques muttered to Roland, "I can get a grimoire, filled with pentagrams and pictures of a goat's head—enough to get the S.I.B. to bring Zack in."

Roland muttered, "For how long?"

Jacques uttered the half-lie, "Very few people return from a meeting with the S.I.B." Very few people did return from meeting with Franco's S.I.B., but the few that did return healthy were very wealthy and connected, like Zack Smithburg.

Jacques followed the half-lie with the words, "We are going to need the help of the Apaches."

Roland's eye lit up with concern at the mention of the organized crime family. The salesman muttered, "The Apaches? Why?"

Jacques said, "How are we going to get the grimoire into Zack's home? Mail it? We need a man experienced in breaking and entering to put the occult stuff in Zack's home."

Roland nodded his head in understanding.

Jacques continued, "I get the grimoire. The Apaches break into Zack's home, place the grimoire under the bed, behind the radio, I don't know. Some place where it's hidden, but not too hidden."

"I call the S.I.B. The investigators show up, find the grimoire, arrest Zack. Zack is gone. The S.I.B. let Smithburg Office Supplies know Zack has been detained."

Roland chimed in, "I step up to the plate, swear myself

in as CEO, and everybody makes out great."

Jacques growled at Roland, "I'll need one thousand pesetas to make this happen."

Roland stuck out his hand, smiled, the criminals shook hands, and a deal was made.

CHAPTER 10

THADEUS MARTIN WAITED IN HIS HIDING PLACE, WATCHED the young lady emerge from the trees and thought, *Easy. This will be easy.* Planning his crime, Thadeus dismissed the advice he had gotten earlier: "Don't mess with the Kannakannack natives. They never forget and they never forgive."

It was 1952 near the Latvia-Sardincia border. The spells August Ording had cast on Thadeus for years had taken their toll. The curses had driven Thadeus from London, across Europe, to the thick forest on the Latvia-Sardincia border, near the guarded border crossing. Curses and dark magick had driven Thadeus to make poor life choice after poor life choice, had driven him from his loving home, had driven him from the arms of his girlfriend Mary, into the life of a thief who lived by his wits.

Thadeus stared out of his one useful eye, the other swollen shut from the beating the Latvia constables had given him the night before. Thadeus knew that unless his latest scam worked, another beating and a matching swollen eye were in his future.

A day earlier, Thadeus had been caught running a three-card monte game on the streets of Riga, the capital of Latvia. As he received his beating from the local cops, Thadeus asked himself, *Why such a vicious beating for such a small crime?*

As the Riga officers threw Thadeus into the back of the police van, the small-time thief had noticed something else. *Watches,* Thadeus had thought, as the van had pulled away from the single room, single story, box-shaped Riga police headquarters, *Riga isn't the capital of Russia or France. It's the capital of a rinky-dink Latvia. But the handful of cops are all flashing solid-gold Rolexes. How do these small-time flatfoots get the long green for the watches?*

The officers had continued beating Thadeus in the back of the van until he had passed out. When Thadeus regained consciousness, the thief lay on his back in a field, the hot sun burning his sore face, his right eye swollen closed, and his head resting on his small suitcase full of trinkets and tchotchkes.

The Sardincian forest, realized the thief. *Those jack-asses drove me to the edge of Latvia, to the Latvia-Sardincia Forest, and then threw me into this field!* Thadeus knew the desertion in the field was a warning, that the officers were saying, "We could have just as easily dropped you into a well, buried you in a hole, or fed you to the forest cougars. This is your last chance. Don't come back."

Staring at the sky, feeling his life couldn't get any worse, the thief felt a lump of dirt crash onto his forehead. Getting to his feet, Thadeus saw two tall and sturdy mercenaries dressed in camouflage and armed with MG-42 machine guns. Thadeus thought, *I'm a criminal who has been chased out of civilized society, but what are two military trained guards doing in the middle of nowhere?*

Determined not to get another punch in the face, Thadeus started to stutter an excuse, an explanation for why he was lying in what was obviously a private field. Before Thadeus could get any words out of his mouth, one of the guards started to spout, "sh-sh-sh-sh-sh," while waving a finger in the universal "Be quiet" gesture.

As Thadeus stood silently, the second guard pointed past Thadeus, to the road back towards the Riga. Thadeus understood the message, "Get as far away from here as quickly as possible."

Knowing a beating was coming if he didn't follow directions, Thadeus picked up his suitcase. As he walked,

Thadeus realized, *I'm on the edge of the Kingdom of Sardincia! A stinking little useless country in the middle of nowhere!*

At that moment, something clicked for Thadeus, a long-forgotten rumor he had heard years ago from soldiers returning home from World War II. *In the Triple Kingdom of Sardincia, there is a valley that has the sweetest, tastiest tobacco found in the world.* Like dominoes, a series of other memories flooded into Thadeus' brain, more recent memories linking with older remembrances. *The infantry coming home from the war raved about the tobacco,* remembered Thadeus, *with some even swearing they would kill for another smoke of it.*

Greed began to weave its way through Thadeus, and half-remembered rumors from drunken nights in bars began to claw their way into his consciousness. Thadeus recalled, *No one could ever get their hands on the mythical Kannakannack tobacco, the smoke that a smart man could sell for thousands in the capitals of Europe!*

Thadeus realized, *The Triple Kingdom of Sardincia is right over the border! The Kannakannack Valley is somewhere in Sardincia!* Thadeus passed a bend in the road and glanced back over his shoulder. The two guards that had chased Thadeus off had joined two other guards at the Latvia-Sardincia crossing. The four guards stood around two wood frame bungalows and a barrier-arm gate. The gate was hung across the dirt road, and was the only thing separating Latvia from the Kingdom of Sardincia. Seeing he was not being watched by the guards, Thadeus looked around to see if there was anyone else nearby. A donkey grazed in a field, but that was all. Thadeus ducked into a shadowed nook to think, within arm's reach of the jennet.

Frustrated that he could be so near to money but unable to figure out how to steal the wealth, an annoyed Thadeus directed his anger at his situation and internally squealed, *What no-talent, half-brained government bureaucrat decided to build the crossing here? What numskull government official randomly chooses a random spot in this god-forsaken forest and says, 'This! This is the official crossing point between Latvia and Sardincia.'*

Just then, a young woman emerged from the forest on the Sardincia side of the border. She wore a bodice that had high, narrow shoulders descending into impossibly tight sleeves, panels that imitated a vest, using a white and green color scheme. The woman wore brown wool pants, large like a man's, held up by suspenders.

Seeing how she was dressed, Thadeus thought, *This woman is dressed from the 1880s.*

As soon as Thadeus saw the large knapsack she carried, Thadeus started to plan. *Look at her grip on that bag,* thought the thief. *She's nervous. That grip on that bag is the grip of a person afraid of having her bag stolen. In a* half-second, Thadeus decided to steal the young woman's bag. *If the mythical tobacco is in that bag, I'm rich! If it's just her lunch, that's almost as good! I'm hungry!*

Thadeus knew that there was a chance the young lady would hand her bag to the guards, that perhaps she was the wife of one of the young men and was bringing dinner, or maybe the guards just demanded a bribe from whoever was passing by. If the young lady handed the bag over, Thadeus would never see any money.

Feeling that his chance to steal the bag was slipping from his hands, and despite engaging in criminal activities in the war, Thadeus had no problem in whispering a prayer to the Lord, "Please, please, please Lord, don't let this girl hand the bag to the guards."

Watching the young lady approach the guarded border-crossing, Thadeus saw his prayer answered. He had built a criminal career watching the actions of potential victims, and as the girl neared the guards, Thadeus thought, *She's never done this before! The expression on her face hasn't changed. There's no warm smile, no recognition in her eyes.*

Thadeus watched the young lady approach the four guards. From his hiding place, Thadeus could see the guards acknowledge the young lady and hear murmurs of a conversation.

Thadeus watched the young lady hold out her passport, neatly folded and closed. She presented her passport in a shy way that indicated to Thadeus that she had never crossed the Sardincian border before, and instead only been told what would happen at the border crossing.

The guards smiled and were friendly, standing around in the way young men do when they are working but wish they weren't, in the way young men do when they are trying to impress a lady but still want to do their job.

The guard that had shushed Thadeus was looking at the young lady's passport. Thadeus saw the slightly perplexed look on the young lady's face and realized she was about to ask something. Thadeus stained to hear.

The young lady asked in Sardincian, "How long a walk to Paris?"

The guards burst out laughing, and the man handling the young lady's passport asked, "Are you half horse?"

From his hiding place, Thadeus saw the look of annoyance on the young lady's face at the guard's words. A wave of glee washed into Thadeus.

Thadeus had been a confidence thief for years and knew the average human wouldn't fall for his scams. But when a person was feeling lonely, falling for scams goes up. As Thadeus saw the disappointment wash over the young girl's face, the thief thought, *I can win this! I can get my hands on that bag she is carrying!*

Thadeus loosened the clasps on his traveling case, led the donkey from the field to the middle of the road, forced his swollen eye open, and stood by the old nag near the edge of the road. He waited until the murmur of conversation between the lady and guards die down. *The border-check is wrapping up. She's coming my way!*

Thadeus knew that ninety-nine times out of a hundred, a person would ignore a stranger in the street. But, if a stranger had been in an accident, even something as simple as a trip and a fall off a donkey, then a person was more than likely to stop and help.

Waiting until the young lady was just turning the bend in the road, so that his activities would be hidden by the guards at the border-crossing, Thadeus took a running leap at the ground. Thadeus timed his actions so it would look as if he had taken a bad fall as he hurried. The trinkets and tchotchkes Thadeus had in his case spilled all over the road.

The young lady reached Thadeus, saw the mess Thadeus was in, and said something in Sardincian Thadeus didn't recognize. Thadeus listened with a confused look, and waited until the young lady asked, "Are you OK?" Thadeus smiled when he heard the lady's thick accent, realizing English was her second language.

Thadeus said to the woman, "Yes! Yes, I am fine!" and then hurriedly struggled to grab all the useless articles, the counterfeit coins and tokens and penny awards he used to lure crowds to his three-card monte game. Thadeus then smiled his most friendliest smile to the young lady and said, "Please, go about your day, don't mind me!"

The young lady said, "Very well, have a good day," and continued on the dirt path.

The young lady's stoic action sent a wave of panic through Thadeus, as he fully expected his target to get on her knees and help pick up his crap. Thadeus blurted in desperation, "Is the border gate to Sardincia on this road?"

The young lady stopped walking away and looked at the thief in the dirt. Thadeus remembered back to when he was a child, in the immediate years after the war, when his Aunt's wealth had vanished and she had taught him to shoplift fruit from the local grocery. "If you are caught, try to picture yourself as a puppy. A helpless puppy that just wants to be loved and taken care of."

Thadeus remembered laughing at his aunt, but when the grocery store cashier had grabbed Thadeus by the upper arm and bellowed, "What did you take?" Thadeus had let the tears fill his eyes and had willed himself to feel like a helpless, lonely puppy. The clerk had let the young Thadeus go.

As an adult in the forest road, desperate to rob, Thadeus willed himself to ooze the helplessness and neediness of a puppy. Thadeus saw a change in the young lady's eyes and thought, *I have her!*

Thadeus started to stammer, "I am so late! And, on top of everything, I must have accidentally rubbed poison ivy on myself!" Thadeus noticed the young lady forcing herself not to giggle.

She stopped walking, picked up some jacks and pick up sticks, and moved to hand the trinkets to Thadeus. When the lady did so, she asked, "Late? For what?"

Stuffing the jacks and sticks into his suitcase, Thadeus said, "Just the most important meeting of my life." Thadeus waited for the lady to ask, "What meeting is that?" but the woman said nothing. Thadeus offered, "I am hoping to buy some tobacco."

The young lady asked, "Tobacco? Do you smoke?"

Thadeus countered, "Me? Not at all!" Thadeus' lie then got more elaborate, a lie designed to make the woman believe she had the upper hand. "I know nothing about tobacco. I'm from Madrid. I sell samples for the chain store I work at." Thadeus could see he was starting to lose the attention of the Sardincian and begged, "Do you know anything about tobacco? I usually don't get assignments like this, but the head trader was out of town, his wife gave birth, and he went back to be with her." Thadeus interrupted himself, so as not to get too tangled in his own lies. "Long story short, I have to make the best of the bad situation."

The woman struggled to hide a smirk.

Thadeus thought, *She thinks I am a moron. Good!* He stood up, looked at his bag, then looked at the young lady, and said, "Wish me luck. I am supposed to convince an experienced Kannakannack trader to trade his bag of valuable Kannakannack tobacco for this load of crap."

The startled young lady whispered, "What?"

"Oh yeah." Thadeus continued to lie. "My boss told me to try and get a case full of the sought-after weed, but at a cheap price, because the Kannakannack people are a bunch of rubes who don't know what they have."

The young lady coldly asked, "When the tobacco trader turns down the case of trinkets, what will you offer?"

Thadeus smiled a big smile and patted the envelope in his chest jacket pocket, the envelope that contained the fake money the street-performer used for sleight of hand. "I've got the cash. I'm ready to pay what the tobacco is really worth, in case the tobacco trader won't be fooled by my line of crap."

The young lady walked close to the con-artist. Thadeus willed every cell of his being to hide the excitement he felt when the woman reached into his jacket pocket and took the envelope full of counterfeit cash.

The woman opened the envelope and, flipping through the counterfeit bills, realized the envelope contained more money than she had ever seen. The young lady said to Thadeus, "Today is your lucky day. My name is Meera. I am willing to make a deal."

Thadeus forced a look of bewilderment to his face. "You? You're selling the weed? I thought I was looking for a guy!"

Smiling, Meera handed her bag full of very valuable tobacco to the slack-jawed Thadeus and said, "I guess you think only guys can negotiate." Tightly gripping the envelope full of fake money, Meera turned away from Thadeus and started to strut back to Sardincia.

Thadeus willed himself to stand still. *Wait,* thought the thief, *wait until she's made the turn in the road, wait until she's out of sight.* When Meera turned down the bend in the road, Thadeus dropped his suitcase, held tight the knapsack with the Kannakannack tobacco, and vaulted onto the donkey.

The nag took off like a rocket, determined to run fast enough to throw Thadeus from its back. Thadeus held on with evil-powered strength. In minutes, the donkey and Thadeus were a mile away.

As Meera walked back to the border-post, she noticed the four guards strangely staring at her. One of the guards silently lifted the arm of the gate, clearing Meera's path. Giving the guards the cold shoulder, Meera strode past, stuffing her envelope full of useless paper into her pocket.

One of the guards asked in Sardincian, "Didn't you have a bag?"

Meera turned, furious that the rude guard would think that he could start to make fun of her again. Meera hissed at the guard in Sardincian, "Yes, I did, but I have sold it, which is better than what you could have done!"

Meera then noticed the looks of confusion and fear on the guards' faces. She demanded in her language, "What? What is the matter?"

A guard fearfully asked in Sardincian, "Miss, would you like to talk about what you got in trade?"

During the next several minutes of awkward conversation, the guards enlightened Meera about con-artists, the bastards that run in the crevices of the world, and counterfeit money.

As the red-faced and embarrassed Meera left the guards and headed back towards the Kannakannack Valley, she hissed, "The bastard thinks he can steal from me. He is wrong."

Chapter 11

Thadeus held the bag of stolen Kannakannack tobacco tight. *I'm not giving up,* thought the thief. *This is my ticket to easy street, and I'm not giving it up, no matter how many men the Apaches send to kill me.*

It was 1952, Spain. Weeks earlier, Thadeus had ridden a stolen donkey to Latvia's only train station, where he hopped on the express to Warsaw. From Warsaw, he went to Paris. From Paris, he went to Madrid. Thadeus had funded his travels by selling small amounts of the Kannakannack tobacco.

In Madrid, Thadeus reached the underworld-famous watering-hole called "Micheal's" where the thief planned to sell the bulk of his precious cargo to Basque separatists.

The Basque separatists, a political party that wanted freedom from Spain, had enough money to buy the tobacco and enough guns not to fear the Apaches. In a brief and whispered conversation with the bartender in the gloomy pub, Thadeus was assured that a criminal contact, an expert in setting up deals, would arrive at the pub in the very late evening. Thadeus enjoyed a pint, snacked on a bowl of free peanuts, and thought, *Finally. Finally my luck is turning around.*

Thadeus became suspicious of his luck when the clock on the wall said 8:55 PM. There was still no sign of his connected criminal that would help him sell his goods, and Thadeus was well aware that the deserted neighborhood surrounding Micheal's made its money robbing lost tourists and weaker criminals.

In the hours that Thadeus had been in the bar, the once-empty pub had become crowded with silent and angry men who radiated violence.

The sun is going down, and the vultures in this town are like vampires. They'll be active at night.

Turning to the bar, Thadeus saw the bartender on the phone. Making eye contact with Thadeus, the bartender mouthed the words "One more?" and gestured as if he pulled another Guinness from the tap.

Thadeus shook his head "No" and got up from the stool, left some bills for the drink on the bar, and grabbed his bag. As he headed for the door, Thadeus called over his shoulder, "I'll be back tomorrow, Aldi, maybe the next day." Thadeus heard the phone receiver get slammed down and the bartender call, "Where you going?"

Thadeus, as a criminal, made it his business to tell civilians off whenever they got mouthy. If a civilian bartender had demanded Thadeus pay for a drink in a club or a civilian bar, Thadeus would either spit at the bartender or curse him out. But when the bartender at Micheal's bellowed for a second time, "Where you going?" Thadeus realized, *I'm not dealing with people that talk things out.*

Thadeus started to stammer, "It's just that it's getting kind of late."

The bar erupted in laughter. A drunk, hidden in the shadows of the bar, bellowed, "Your mommy want you home before dark?" and the laughter started up again.

A patron of the pub grabbed for Thadeus' bag. Thadeus pulled the bag close to himself and stared at the grabby man as the crowd uttered a loud, "Ohhhhh!"

The bartender started at Thadeus for a quarter minute, then waved Thadeus over. Intimidated, the young thief walked back to the bar. Aldi, the bartender, said, "You are causing a lot of trouble. You think meeting this guy is easy?"

Oh no, thought Thadeus.

"You're the big guy on campus. He's going to drop everything and come to meet you? Some clown that claims he's got a bagful of Kannakannack tobacco?"

Thadeus realized he could get mugged, started to stammer an excuse, but was cut off.

"You know how many pansies come in here, day in and day out, wanting to sell some plant that they claim is Kannakannack tobacco?"

At this time, Jacques Proust sat in a corner nook of the bar. Hidden in shadows, his back to the excitement, Jacques listened to hear what would happen next.

"Know what? Go. Get out of here. I don't need your baloney. But if you go, there's no meeting with the buyer. Ever," Jacques heard Aldi the bartender say.

Thadeus sat down on his bar stool. The bartender pulled another pint and placed it in front of Thadeus as a conciliatory gesture.

Sipping his drink, Thadeus asked, *Why isn't anyone making fun of me? After a dressing down, some drunk jerk always continues the bullying.*

Thadeus looked around. The men were either looking at their drinks, staring into space, or glaring at the floor. *Everyone is avoiding eye contact,* realized Thadeus, *and not just with me. They can't even look at each other.*

The clock struck nine and started to chime. The large, overweight pale man hissed, "Christ" through clenched teeth and stumbled-ran back to his seat. Thadeus heard the clip-clop of a horse-drawn carriage.

The bartender joked, "The good Father is here boys. Now, who wants to join the monks?" The barflies in the pub forced a laugh at the joke they had heard a dozen times before.

The clip-clop stopped. Thadeus stared at the door. As the silence of the bar somehow got even more intense, Thadeus strained to listen, just as he had years ago in the shelter in London.

Thadeus heard a hurried shuffle and saw Ording enter the bar. *Oh no,* thought Thadeus, as he recognized the small man from the night in the London Tunnel. There wasn't a stitch of fat or muscle on the five-foot tall man's frame. Other than the sprinkling of a few gray hairs, the little man hadn't aged a day.

The men in the bar moved away from Thadeus, the men in the center of the bar leaving their seats and pushing up against those who were seated or stood by the wall.

Thadeus tried to run, but the bartender grabbed Thadeus from behind, pinning Thadeus' arm against the bar, forcing Thadeus' head against the wall by the back of the neck.

When Ording saw Thadeus, a huge smile broke out over the occultist's face.

Aldi demanded, "Well? Is this the guy?"

Ording smiled and said, "Yes. Yes, this is the guy."

Ording turned in Thadeus' direction. "I've been

expecting you. I had a vision that you would show up here, but I wasn't 100% sure until I saw you in the flesh!" whispered the occultist. "It's been years! It is good to see you!" Thadeus saw Ording's smile drain away and heard the priest growl, "I'm guessing that the ear infection that saved you last time is all gone. Let's get you back into the game."

Thadeus made another effort to break free and run, but the patrons of the bar joined the hands of the bartender. "You're not going anywhere," he heard someone growl.

Thadeus saw the patron pull back his arm, chambering a punch. The man's blow hit Thadeus across the jaw. Thadeus slung into unconsciousness.

When Thadeus blinked himself awake, he was in a small room, laying on a thin cot, with Ording standing and staring at him.

Ording smiled as he said, "Welcome to the fight. Your transformation starts now."

CHAPTER 12

Meera stood outside Diego's Tabaco Emporio and thought, *I won't make the same mistake I made in Posnan.*

It was 1952 in Madrid, Spain. Meera knew the thief that had stolen from her was in the city, but Meera also knew she needed cash to continue the hunt. Meera planned to sell some of her Kannakannack tobacco in Spain's thriving tobacco community.

Spain had imported tobacco from Morocco since the 1600s, with tobacco sales and trade becoming a thriving business. Spanish tobacco shops, or Tabacos, provided the smoking connoisseur a variety of tobacco similar to what the well-stocked bar provided the alcohol enthusiast.

In 1952, the laws regulating what people could and

couldn't smoke hadn't been written.

What was a problem for Meera in 1952 was Dictator Franco's squad of morality enforcers, the Social Investigation Brigade. After seizing control in 1933, Franco had rolled back the legal rights of women to only those rights stipulated in the 1889 Napoleonic Code. Women needed their brother's, father's, or husband's permission to perform an array of basic, but male-defined, activities. Those activities included applying for a job, opening a bank account, or shopping for tobacco.

Meera walked into Diego's Tabacos as the siesta ended and the evening began, surprising the group of tobacco enthusiasts as their night-time routine started. As the door to the Tabacos shop closed behind Meera, the scent of the different strains and leaves of tobacco rushed towards the Sardincian. Broadleaf mixed with the scent of Burley, Thuoc Lao mixed with the scent of Perique. The beautiful aroma was strong as Meera told herself she had come to the right place, that a good decision had been made.

The group that haunted the Tabaco was made up of tall, short, fat, skinny, dim-witted, and intelligent men, a diverse group united in their love to smoke. The group was startled when Meera walked in the door, silenced by surprise and fear.

The men in the Tabacos weren't priests. At least half had broken some of the multitude of overlapping and contradictory laws the Dictator of Spain had imposed on his country. Seeing a young lady in a restricted area made every member of the group wary, and at least one asked himself, "Is today the day? The day the brigade comes for me?"

The men puffed on their respective choice of smoke, which varied between cigarette, cigar, and pipe, and waited for something to happen.

A large, heavy man, sitting on a tall stool and having the air of a leader, called to Meera, "Can I help you, miss? Are you interested in tobacco? A gift for a boyfriend? Your father?" The man chose his words carefully.

In Franco's Spain, there was a court system. The court system was designed to find and punish anyone who criticized Franco, but there was the rare occasion where a civilian who broke one of Franco's laws avoided jail. Avoiding jail was simple, if Franco or his minions didn't have a personal grudge against the accused. Just pay the bribe and have something that the defense could use. Asking a woman if she was running an errand for her father was a question that would save a railroaded businessman jail time.

Meera, not quite understanding the mannerisms of the Spanish but knowing little said was easy mended, replied in Spanish dripping in a Sardincian accent, "Yes, a gift." Meera then took out a diluted Kannakannack cigarette.

Meera had learned that straight Kannakannack tobacco

was too strong for inexperienced Kannakannack tobacco users, so she had mixed a portion of her village's tobacco with some American cigarette tobacco. Holding up her hand-rolled cigarette, Meera asked, "Can I interest you in some Kannakannack smoke?"

Except for the large proprietor of the store, the group burst out laughing.

The idea of the S.I.B. sending a woman to sell something as rare and valuable as Kannakannack to entrap a group of everyday men struck the tobacconists as absurd.

One of the Tabaco customers muttered, "Is this real?" which was a polite way of saying, "What is the crazy foreigner on about?"

Another customer mistook Meera's Sardincian accent for the similar sounding Russian and growled, "Careful. She's a Russki."

The owner of the store pretended not to hear the chatter of the crowd and asked, "Can I take a look?"

Meera handed her Kannakannack/American cigarette to the man.

The crowd got silent. Some of the men stubbed out their cigarettes, their pipes, their cigars in preparation for a new type of thrill. Their addiction to tobacco and their physical need for a new high outweighed their fear of the S.I.B. The customers crowded around what Meera had handed over.

The proprietor took out a handkerchief as white as

snow and laid the handkerchief on the counter. The proprietor took Meera's cigarette and unrolled the paper, intent on checking the contents of what Meera was offering. The contents of the cigarette fell on a white kerchief, and Diego of Diego's Tabaco leaned over the counter, his hands appearing to rest in his lap, hidden from view.

The crowd peered over the shoulders of the proprietor. A less inexperienced smoker muttered, "Looks like Kentucky Burly, nothing special."

A second later, as Diego spread the small cuttings of mixed tobacco over the handkerchief, he gasped, "Meirda!" Others in the group quickly followed suit, their eyes registering a small cutting of a leaf they had never seen before.

As the entire crowd was staring at the small pile of mixed tobacco on the store counter, Diego covertly pressed a button with his foot. The button, hidden in the floor beneath the store's counter, caused a light to flash in the store's back room. Diego's young nephew looked up from the game of solitaire he had been playing.

In the front room of the store, Diego took a pair of tweezers from his shirt pocket and grasped a larger cutting of a Kannakannack leaf. Diego muttered, "A match? Has anyone a match?" Half-a-dozen lit matches appeared. Diego grabbed the closest and lit the small square of Kannakannack weed to test how the weed would burn.

The plant burned slowly, elegantly. The musky, unique

smoke curled in the air. The group of aficionados wasn't certain it was Kannakannack tobacco, but they were certain what was in front of them was unique.

Diego turned back to the small pile of tobacco in front of him. A customer next to Diego, obviously some type of confident to the shop owner, murmured, "Maybe 30%? 30% of the pile is the unique weed."

Another customer hissed, "Dump it all into hookah, we can have a taste."

Yet another customer reached to grasp a small cutting, but Diego slapped the customer's hand away.

Having determined that there was a uniqueness in Meera's cigarette, Diego asked, "Do you have more?"

Meera lied and said, "Two more."

Diego asked, "When can you get more?"

Meera replied, "I can't say."

Diego thought for a moment, then said, "I will buy all three cigs."

Meera produced two more of her tainted cigarettes and explained to the group, "When smoking, dim the lights. Play a soft beat. The experience will be positive."

Meera made a substantial profit from the sale, enough to live well in Madrid for some time. From the money he was willing to pay, Meera knew Diego hadn't seen true Kannakannack tobacco before.

Diego took all three cigarettes, and with the help of

the other enthusiasts, carefully isolated the Kannakannack tobacco from the American. Diego planned to smoke the weed in a hookah, giving anyone who could pay the steep price of entry a chance to experience the unique smoke.

When Meera left the store, Diego shook Meera's hand and cooed, "It has been a pleasure. I hope to do business with you again. Come back soon."

Meera left the Tabaco Emporio feeling rich and unaware she was being followed by Diego's nephew, a gangster named Top-Hat.

CHAPTER 13

Roxanne O'Brien remembered the welts and bruises on her son and swore, *Things are going to change.*

It was 1952 in Madrid. Roxanne O'Brien, wife of Smithburg Office Supplies C.E.O. Roland O'Brien, stood outside the locked door of her husband's office. She listened to the loud drunk snoring of her husband and the raucous laughter of Roland's violent friends.

Days ago, Roxanne finally had enough of her husband's crap and decided to get a divorce. Under the Caudillo of Spain's fascist government, divorce was illegal, but Roxanne had learned of Ms. Perez-Sanchez.

Ms. Perez-Sanchez was a triple-divorced lawyer, a freedom-fighter for those bound in the chains of matrimony.

Ms. Perez-Sanchez had a team of lawyers in London that could guarantee a divorce, given a few days and a small percentage of the marriage settlement. A legal divorce in London would be upheld by the courts of Spain.

Roxanne had been raised to believe divorce was one of the most heinous of all sins. The Sisters of Poverty, the Catholic organization that dominated the educational system of rural Zahara, tolerated no foolishness, no mistakes, and no questioning about what was a sin and what wasn't. "Didn't do the homework? Is it because you are stupid?" or "Holding hands with a boy? You're the type that welcomed the Axis, aren't you?" were the type of reprimands from the Sisters, the type of insult disguised as a question, the type of admonishment that brought shame.

Roxanne lived a life that minimized her unhappiness while remaining married. Roland got drunk, hung out with gangsters, and had affairs. Roxanne made sure she spent as little time as possible with her second husband, Roland, and that Stephon, her son with her first husband, had the best education possible.

Most nights Roxanne slept next to her son. Some nights Roxanne woke up from the noise of Roland's associates echoing through the home. On the nights where Roxanne was startled awake by drunken rumbling, she thanked the Lord that the door to her son's room was locked.

There was a night when Roxanne was startled awake

by the creaking and clicking of the door-knob to her son's room—a sure sign someone was trying to get in. When Roxanne heard a drunk Apache ask, "Roland, my man, have you the key?" and Roland answered, "Nah, man, the stupid realtor never gave me all the keys to this place." Roxanne remembered, *Thank God for Ella and her short-changing Roland's set of keys.*

Roxanne often asked herself what she could have done differently. Roxanne cursed Franco's men and her husband's death in prison. Roxanne cursed the day she had seen Smithburg Corporation's "Help Wanted" ad in the daily paper.

Roxanne cursed herself for not heeding the warnings of Mrs. Eleana-Goode, the Human Resources Director at Smithburg that had warned against interoffice dating.

Anger built in Roxanne when she told herself, again and again, *Roland changed after we got married! Ever since he became C.E.O. of Smithburg, he's gotten even more drunk than usual! His new friends are jackasses!*

Roland's new friends were members of the Apaches, a Paris-based crime organization. Roxanne endured the snide comments from her husband and the Apaches, but when Roxanne saw the bruises on her son's arm, Roxanne vowed to make changes.

It was Mrs. Gloria Sanchez, H.R. Director of Smithburg, who let Roxanne know how to pursue a divorce. After

Roland became C.E.O., on one of the few days when Roxanne was in the office, Mrs. Gloria Sanchez asked to see Roxanne. When Roxanne walked into Mrs. Gloria Sanchez's office, Roxanne noticed how pale Gloria Sanchez appeared, that there was even a slight quiver in Gloria Sanchez's voice.

Mrs. Gloria Sanchez began, "Mrs. O'Brien, ever since Mr. O'Brien took over as C.E.O., there have been irregularities. All the new young men that Mr. O'Brien has hired as consultants have been," at this point Mrs. Gloria Sanchez paused, trying to find a different word than "harassing . . ."

Mrs. Gloria Sanchez continued, ". . . have been dating the young professional ladies." At this point, Mrs. Gloria Sanchez paused again and took a deep breath before continuing. "I'm resigning, but I wanted to make sure you had all the information about your options." At this point, Mrs. Gloria Sanchez slid Roxanne the business card of Ms. Perez-Sanchez, Madrid's infamous divorce lawyer. Days later, Roxanne vowed she would use Ms. Perez-Sanchez's services when she caught the Apaches man-handling her son.

It was the middle of the afternoon. Roland was drunk and sitting incoherently on the living room couch while his Apache friends listened to sports on the radio and used the house phone to place bets. Roxanne had picked up her son, Stephon, from day care and was taking him to their pool back when Stephon asked, "Where is my baseball?"

Roxanne told her son to sit and wait for the two minutes it would take her to fetch his toy.

Taking a short-cut to Stephon's room, Roxanne caught one of the Apaches trying to jimmy open the door to her husband's private office, the office where Roland O'Brien kept the family's financial records. Roxanne said, "Why don't you ask Roland for the key?"

The Apache turned to face Roxanne and hissed in his French-accented Spanish, "Roland is passed out on the couch beneath that framed painting of Majorca. Your husband is so drunk he can't even remember where he left the key, baby."

Roxanne felt her face turn red with anger when she heard the thug say, "baby."

Roxanne hissed, "I want you out of my house!"

The Apache slowly turned on his heel and started walking toward the exit. "Sure," whispered the Apache. "See you tomorrow." Roxanne retrieved her son's ball and stormed out of the home.

After her husband passed out on the couch the next day, the two Apaches visited the backyard where Roxanne isolated herself with her boy. The Apaches insisted on clowning around, joking with her boy, hiding their cruelty behind a mask of friendly roughhousing. Roxanne knew the Apaches' actions were punishment for her speaking up.

The Apaches started asking Stephon about the girls in his school, who he liked, who the sluts were, was the girl he liked a whore. The Apaches threw Stephon into the pool, grabbing him so hard bruises showed on his arm.

Roxanne screamed at the Apaches to leave or she would call the police. The Apaches left, joking to Stephon that his mother was cold, saying they would leave but they would be back to play tomorrow.

The day after she screamed at the Apaches, Roxanne O'Brien stood outside the exclusive Metropolis Building. The Metropolis Building was one of the various ultra-busy five story commercial buildings circling Madrid's Plaza De Sol. As the crowd of office workers hustled to and from work, Roxanne mentally and emotionally prepared herself to meet with Ms. Perez-Sanchez.

Roxanne assumed her meeting with Ms. Perez-Sanchez would start with a lecture just like the nuns used to deliver. The lecture never came. Ms. Perez-Sanchez only asked Roxanne to explain how she met her husband.

"When I saw the ad in the paper that Smithburg Office Supplies was looking for administrative assistants, I applied for the job," said Roxanne.

Roxanne paused, waiting for Ms. Perez-Sanchez to break into an angry diatribe. Ms. Perez-Sanchez said nothing.

"I had been working at Smithburg only two weeks,"

said Roxanne. "Everything was fine until I met Roland. It was the first night I was working late, and I didn't understand what I was asked to do!"

Ms. Perez-Sanchez spoke, "Didn't understand? Could you expand on that?"

Roxanne stuttered, "The company had given us a week's worth of training, and I paid attention, but I am positive what was dumped on my desk wasn't covered in the training."

Ms. Perez-Sanchez asked, "Was it your supervisor who gave you the project?"

Roxanne muttered, "It was the Head of Sales. The man who would become my husband."

Ms. Perez-Sanchez stated, "So you met your hubby when he gave you, out of the blue, out of the chain of command, some work assignment."

Roxanne continued, "Of course, I messed it up. I didn't know what I was doing."

Ms. Perez-Sanchez asked, "That is the night your future husband first asked you out for drinks?"

Roxanne nodded her head in a "Yes" gesture.

Roxanne waited as Ms. Perez-Sanchez scribbled something on a notepad, still waiting for the lecture to start. Ms. Perez-Sanchez said nothing, did not start a lecture. Ms. Perez-Sanchez just asked, "Would you like to continue?"

Roxanne gave the answer she had been conditioned to

give, Roxanne gave the self-blaming answer she believed she was required to give. "I shouldn't have agreed to after-work drinks. I shouldn't have . . ." Roxanne's voice trailed off, as she wasn't exactly sure what had been required of her.

Ms. Perez-Sanchez confronted Roxanne. "Shouldn't have what? What shouldn't you have done?"

Roxanne said nothing, unsure of what her next words were. Hearing Roxanne's pause, Ms. Perez-Sanchez finally started to lecture. It was a type of lecture Roxane had never heard before.

"Roxanne, you're the wronged party here," Ms. Perez-Sanchez said. "Your husband has been playing with you from the beginning. Breaking your confidence by giving you an assignment that couldn't be completed. That you hadn't been trained in. By browbeating you into drinks. By using his position to intimidate you into drinks. You deserve justice. And compensation."

Confidence surged in Roxanne as she thought, *Finally! Finally someone is taking my side!*

"The drawback to my system is you need to have the marriage's bank account information to get your money," Ms. Perez-Sanchez said to Roxanne.

Roxanne bit her lip in concern.

"Roxanne, the financials I'm asking to see? The money is your money. Your husband will insist it's his money, but he's wrong. You do know that? Can you get your financial paperwork?"

Roxanne nodded her head, whispered, "Yes," and thought, *The paperwork is in Roland's locked office.*

Ms. Perez-Sanchez said, "We could get a writ from the court forcing your husband to hand over financials, but that could take years." A smile crept onto Ms. Perez-Sanchez's face. "I find it's better to grab the money, and then make the husband try to claw it back. And fail!"

Roxanne nodded in agreement.

Ms. Perez-Sanchez pressed a button on her phone and said, "Could you send Paul in?"

A very fit middle-aged man whose hair was turning a salt-and-pepper gray named Paul Kanie walked into the office.

Ms. Perez-Sanchez asked, "Paul, Ms. O'Brien needs a lift to pick up some paperwork. Could you see that it happens?"

Paul nodded and said, "Sure."

Paul drove Roxanne home. As he drove, he said, "I'm a retired boxer."

Roxanne thought, *Is this old man trying to impress me? I've had enough of old men. That's why I'm getting a divorce.*

Paul continued, "Whenever I was nervous about a fight, I'd picture in my mind how I was going to win. Literally. I'd picture myself walking into the ring, seeing the opponent, seeing the opponent swing, miss, then eat my fist."

Roxanne thought, *What the heck is this guy talking about?*

Paul calmly continued, "Picturing yourself winning is where it all starts, miss. But if you can't picture your new life after the big win, then how can you ask anyone else to picture it?"

Roxanne thought, *This guy sounds like he is on my side.*

Paul said, "I'm going to park two blocks away from the house, in case anyone is home."

Roxanne grudging said, "Fine," and thought, *Fat lot of good that does me.*

After parking the car, Paul held out a whistle to Roxanne. "If there is any trouble at all, just blow. I'll be there in two shakes of a lamb's tail!" Paul pulled up his untucked, loose-fitting button-down shirt and revealed a small revolver.

Roxanne took the whistle, then quickly and quietly approached her home. Roxanne counted on the carousing of the Apaches, the drunken stupor of her husband, and the fact that she had snuck up on foot instead of driving up in her car to go unnoticed. As Roxanne approached her home, she thought, *Thank God daycare is letting Stephon stay late.*

Entering her home through the back way, knowing that the Apaches probably listened for the splashing of her son to announce that she was home, Roxanne quietly pulled back the sliding door to the kitchen. Roxanne heard the voices of the Apache gang members.

Roxanne thought, *They are in the front. Good. They don't know I am here. They don't know!* Roxanne jumped in surprise and almost squealed in panic when she heard the loud "THUMP" against the parlor wall of her home, the loud crash that followed, and then a cheer of the gangsters.

Roxanne almost turned and ran, but didn't. She listened but didn't hear the pounding of feet or the stomping of the gangsters. Roxanne continued to listen, and heard the Apaches joke, "Dang! The painting!"

They are throwing my son's ball against the walls, doing damage for no reason. Roxanne started to tip-top to the laundry room. The room Roland never saw or knew existed.

When Ella, the real estate agent, had given Roland the keys to the home, Roland had rudely grabbed the keys and ran inside as he shouted, "This is the only set?"

Ella had pleasantly shouted back to Roland, "Of course!" The agent had then whispered to Roxanne, "Your husband has all the keys he needs, the keys to the front door and his office. In case you ever need to surprise the man, as wives sometimes need to, check behind the washing machine."

Ella knew Roland was a bastard from the start.

Listening to the thump of the Apaches throw the ball against the parlor wall, Roxanne reached behind her home's washing machine. Roxanne stretched to a hidden cubby-hole and grasped a small bag. In the bag were keys to all the locks in the house, including the locks to Roland's home office.

Though frightening, the thumping of the ball against the various walls of the home worked in her favor. Listening to the thumps, Roxanne thought, *They are on the move. They are stomping up the stairs.*

Roxanne quietly ran down the hallway to her husband's office. Her hands shaking, Roxanne found the correct key, put it in the lock, turned it, flung open the door, stepped inside, and quietly shut the door to Roland's office.

Roxanne let her eyes adjust to the dimness of Roland's private room. There was a musty, unpleasant smell from somewhere in the room, because a drunk Roland had left a forgotten ham sandwich to rot in a hidden crevice.

Roxanne heard a loud bang from upstairs, as an Apache had taken aim at some object upstairs and decided it was a target. The bang was followed by a crash, laughter, and some loud words that Roxanne couldn't distinguish. *Good,* thought Roxanne, *The bastards are in my bedroom.* Roxanne turned her attention to Roland's desk.

Roland's roll-top vintage desk was half-hidden in the mid-size room, made dark and gloomy with heavy drawn shades. Mountains of boxes, paper, and office knick-knacks stacked every which way crowded out the space in the office, leaving only the thinnest of paths to Roland's desk.

Next to Roland's desk sat an open safe, half hidden under a pile of paper. But there was nothing in there. He'd spent a fortune getting the safe installed and then forgot the combination.

Roxanne heard the Apaches again, the tone of their voice getting louder, like a disagreement.

Pushing other concerns out of her mind, Roxanne viewed the hoarder-like pile of garbage that surrounded her husband's desk and asked herself, *Why would Roland have all this crap?*

Because he's a thief. Roland's a thief, and like all thieves, he is waiting for the day when someone steals from him. He thinks this load of receipts and notes will help get what is stolen from him back.

Looking at the useless safe and piles of paper, Roxanne thought, *The info I need must be in the desk.*

As Roxanne made her way to the half-buried roll-top secretary, she heard a burst of laughter from upstairs, then the sounds of men roughhousing. Roxanne went back to searching for the paperwork that would give her access to her money.

Roland's desk was heavy, thick-wooded, with a roll-top and intricate designs on its legs and sides. Roxanne grabbed the handle of the roll-top and pushed up the rolling cover. Bundles of paper cascaded from the desk to the office floor with a soft crash.

Roxanne held her breath, waiting and listening for any indication that the thumping of bundled paper against the office floor had been heard.

Roxanne heard the mumbling of the Apaches from upstairs. Then she heard the ball bounce, hard, followed by another bounce. And then another bounce. The bounces were coming closer. *They are upstairs, and bouncing the ball against the floor as they walk around.*

Roxanne waited and listened. The sound of the bouncing ball stayed upstairs.

Roxanne grabbed at the paper on the floor, some of the bundles wrapped tight with rubber bands, other stacks held together with paperclips, some loose sheets stuffed with other unrelated sheets of paper into unrelated folders. Some of the receipts had cryptic notes, scribbled with Roland's indecipherable handwriting.

The information I need isn't on any of these scraps of paper. My husband is a disorganized mess, but even he must know how important the banking info is. Roland must keep the info somewhere safe but easy to get to.

Somewhere hidden but easy to get to.

Feeling foolish, but knowing she was right, Roxanne got down on her knees and felt around the bottom edge of the desktop.

While on her knees was when Roxanne realized the

sound of the bouncing ball had stopped. Roxanne listened and could hear the murmur of the Apaches from upstairs. Suddenly Roxanne heard a burst of laughter and the rush of footsteps.

They are running for the stairs, Roxanne realized.

There was the sound of a shuffle. The Apaches had started some type of shoving match at the type of the stairs. Roxanne heard the soft quick sounds of the dropped baseball bouncing down a flight of stairs. She heard the ball reach the bottom of the stairs, then clatter as it bounced in random directions. Roxanne then heard the ball settled on a direction and bounce down the hall.

The hall right outside Roland's office door.

Panic ran through Roxanne. *The door! Did I lock the door?* Roxanne put the whistle to her lips, took a deep breath, got ready to blow, and then stopped herself.

I haven't found the money papers yet.

Roxanne tip-toe-ran to the office door. Roxanne could hear the Apaches push and shove each other, playing the game so many boys play, trying to get the object when the friend is keeping it away. Roxanne reached to grab the door handle, to make sure the door was locked, when the door shook with a loud bang.

An Apache had thrown himself against the door, blocking the other from getting the ball. *If I lock the door now, will they notice the click from the hall?*

Roxanne heard the clicking of the doorknob and realized one of the Apaches checked the office door. The locked door didn't open.

Roxanne heard an Apache say, "Let's see what's in the fridge," and his companion comment, "Sure!" and observe, "I like it when Roland ditches us for Sophia. Gives us the run of the place."

Hearing the name "Sophia" only firmed her resolve.

Roxanne went back to the desk. In seconds, Roxanne had found the button to the secret compartment that contained a very nice and neat list of all the monetary assets of Roland in the banks of London, Madrid, and Paris.

Roxanne grabbed the lists and a small duffel bag that had something heavy inside, shoved the lists into the bag, closed the door to the compartment, jammed all the paper that had spilled onto the floor from the roll-top earlier back into the desk's enclosure, and shut the roll-top.

Then she waited. Roxanne waited until the laughter from the kitchen died down, until the sound of boys drinking beer as they ate chicken salad died down, until she heard the sound of drowsy well fed-boys get up from their mid-day feeding, until the sound of boys stumbling to nap in parlor armchairs was heard. Then Roxanne opened the office door and tip-toed out the building's front door, praying that Paul hadn't driven away.

Paul hadn't. He just asked, "Any problems?"

Roxanne was in too good of a mood to say anything other than, "None that I couldn't handle."

Paul grinned and said, "So you visualized your success?"

Roxanne snapped, "Oh, will you just drive, Paul?" Roxanne wanted to get away from her old life, for good, as quickly as possible.

CHAPTER 14

Jacques Proust unlocked and opened the door to his apartment, jumping with surprise when he saw Mr. Brett sitting on his couch.

It was 1952 in Madrid. Jacques had been recruited as an informant for Madrid's Social Investigation Brigade.

Mr. Brett sat reclined on the couch, as comfortable as if he were in his own apartment. The agent was drinking Jacques' sangria, had a briefcase open next to him, and was reading a report. When Jacques walked in and jumped with surprise, Mr. Brett ignored Jacques' reaction and said, "Jacques, finally you're here. You do take your time getting home from work, don't you?"

Jacques stammered, "I didn't know you'd be here."

Mr. Brett said nothing. The agent just threw the papers he was reading in his briefcase, pulled out a bronze medallion, threw the paper-weight-sized trinket on Jacques' coffee table, and said, "Hide that, will you?"

Jacques picked up the talisman and asked, "Where did you get this?"

Mr. Brett asked, "A lady named Roxanne O'Brien is getting a divorce and found this in her husband's belongings. Roxanne talked to her lawyer about it. Ms. Perez-Sanchez called us, because any occult artifacts need to be turned over to the SIB."

Jacques asked, "What is it?"

Mr. Brett snapped his briefcase closed and answered, "It's the *Jomhuri-ye Eslâmi-ye* Amulet, and it belongs to the British. Since it belongs to Queen Elizabeth, it can't stay in any official safe in Spain. So, you will keep it . . . for now."

Jacques asked himself, *What am I getting into?* before deciding to hide the amulet behind the stove in the kitchen.

CHAPTER 15

Meera sat at the cafe and watched the young man that had been following her.

It was 1952 in Madrid. In her travels, Meera had lost any naivete. She walked the streets of Europe with her eyes open and ears listening, as alert as when she walked in the cougar-infested Sardincian forest of her homeland.

Minutes after selling a small sample of her Kannakannack tobacco, Meera the Hunter had realized a man had been following her. Growing tired of being followed, Meera sat down in a cafe on a crowded street, ordered a coffee and a newspaper, and waited.

After thirty minutes of pretending to read a newspaper and surreptitiously watching the young man as he stood on a corner across from where she sat, Meera knew she was not imagining anything. He was following her.

After forty minutes of pretending to read her newspaper, Meera looked up and smiled at the man. The young man smiled back. Meera waved at the man, inviting him over. The young man trotted over to Meera.

"Hi," said Meera, with a smile.

Leaning in close, with a big smile on his face, the young man cooed, "Hey, cutie."

Meera asked, "What's your name?"

The young man said, "My friends call me Top-Hat."

Leaving cash on the table to pay for her drink and tip the waiter, Meera said in her most pleasant voice, "Top-Hat, have you heard of a young man selling Kannakannack tobacco?"

Top-Hat lied, "Sure, baby, I got a truckload of the stuff. I got a team of people bringing the stuff in. How much you need?"

Meera knew right away that Top-Hat was full of baloney and said, "Could you quit following me? You're not very good at it."

The smile disappeared from Top-Hat's face, replaced with a mask of anger.

Meera turned and left, confident that the boy would sulk away. In Kannakannack, when a boy was told by a lady that she wasn't interested, the boy took the hint.

Top-Hat wasn't a Kannakannack boy. He was an Apache gangster who took embarrassment personally. Watching Meera walk away, the gangster vowed retribution.

Top-Hat, by word-of-mouth, sent a message to the minions and low-level gangsters eager to do violence. "There is a lady about, dressed like a Kannakannack hillbilly. Pursue and drive her to the boatyards." At the boatyards, there were few police, and the Apaches were the law.

The message spread like wild-fire among the Apaches.

As Meera went from bar to bar, pub to pub, and nightclub to nightclub, searching for the thief that had stolen from her, she noticed the men that peeked at her from street corners and out of doorways. Meera tried to avoid the men. But as she noticed more and more men staring at her, half-hidden, Meera realized, *The little boy I gave the 'get lost' warning to has decided he is a tough guy. And he's bringing his friends to play.*

Meera picked up on the fact that the boys were trying to herd her towards the Puerta Del Sol waterway.

Fine, thought Meera, *You bastards may think you're trapping me on the docks. You're not. I'm trapping you.*

CHAPTER 16

MEERA THE SARDINCIAN STOOD ON THE DOCKS OF THE Puerta Del Sol shipping port and thought, *I'm not going to die here, in a strange country at the hands of criminals.*

It was 1952 in Madrid. Meera had a satchel full of valuable Kannakannack tobacco stolen from her, and the determined Sardincian had pursued the thief from Latvia, to Bonn, to Warsaw, to Paris, and finally to Madrid. In Madrid, Meera became the target of the gangster Top-Hat.

Top-Hat scoured the city, his associates and minions playing a cat-and-mouse game with Meera. In a strange city, hunted, Meera camouflaged herself next to a packing crate, hidden in the shadows. Meera took three deep breaths, calmed herself, and waited for her pursuers. Then, on the docks of the Puerta del Sol, Meera heard a deep voice start to sing.

An orchestra joined the singing. Meera followed the music through the maze of stacked shipping crates to a hidden theatrical performance. The Teatro Real Company was performing a private rendition of Anton Rubinstein's "Demon."

Meera found a stage with performers, a traveling orchestra, and a crowd milling about in front of the stage. A small bar served drinks while waiters in tuxedos bought hors d'oeuvres to the Dior, Givenchy, and Chanel clad crowd. There was a tent set up in the cordoned off area where the delicious smell of roasted pork emanated. A large man, over two hundred pounds and nearly six feet tall, laughed a loud laugh while talking to a bevy of ladies and sycophants. The performers, staff, and attendees were hemmed in by a row of large men and tiki torches.

The crowd attending the opera was made of bohemians and cultural nomads, of young inheritors of vast wealth, of young scions that were addicted to finding the next new thrill. The thrill in Madrid, in the 1950s, was occultism.

Meera noticed the large men surrounding the crowd all faced outward, towards the docks that were piled high with crates and boxes of all shapes and sizes, and realized, *Security. The big men are security for the entertainers and crowd.*

Around Meera, with the darkness rolling into Madrid, dangerous men materialized out from the ether. Men with alcohol problems, men with substance abuse problems, large men with anger issues, all came alive as night fell. The broken men woke from their hiding places, crawling from the nooks and crannies where they wasted the days of their life, from between the stacked crates, to attack the night and grab whatever they could from whoever they could. All the men were aligned with Top-Hat, and all the men were looking for Meera.

Hunters of the Kannakannack Valley could stand as still as a statue for hours, breathing so shallow even the easily startled Sardincian pigeon would alight within centimeters. As Meera stood perfectly still waiting for the bohemian's security to drop their vigilance, knowing that inside the spectacle's guards there was safety, she felt movement behind her.

Meera didn't move when she heard the creaking of wood. She just thought, *Thugs with footsteps so heavy would never be able to hunt the Kannakannack deer.* Meera felt breathing inches away from her neck. *Top-Hat heard the music, the same as me.*

Meera heard the scratch of a match against a striker, saw a sudden explosion of light, and then heard a bitter "Put that out!"

It was the voice of her adversary, as he commanded one

of his flunkies to put out the match that would have been used to light a cigarette.

Top-Hat knows I'm near.

Meera dived towards the security guards into the circle of light cast by the tiki torches.

As Meera approached the crowd, one of the plains-clothes security guards held up his hand to indicate that Meera should come no closer and asked, "Can I help you?"

Meera recalled a club in Warsaw, when she was still learning the peculiarities of Western Europe, how the doorman had let her enter just because she was a female.

The large, plain clothes security guard asked again, "Can I help you?"

Behind her, in the dark, Meera heard Top-Hat hiss, "Hey baby, you thought you dodged me, didn't you?"

The bohemian's security guard snapped his head towards the sound and grabbed for the weapon under his jacket as he peered into the dark.

A wave of concern washed through Meera when she heard another voice hiss from the darkness of the docs, "This time he brought good friends." The hiss was followed by a perverted giggle.

The large security man for the bohemians peered into the darkness, hearing but not seeing Top-Hat and his crew of troublemakers. After a beat, the large man stopped staring, turned and glared at Meera, and said, "Get out of here."

Uh-oh, thought Meera. From the giggle fit of Top-Hat's minions, Meera guessed there were at least five low-level thug Apaches surrounding Top-Hat. The dumb thugs were useful for little besides breaking open crates on piers and holding down a victim as another Apache rained down blows.

The security guard repeated, "Get out of here. Now!"

Meera was left dumb-founded, unsure of how to plead her case, when she heard a female voice pipe-up from behind the large guard, "She's with us."

Meera peered around the huge guard and saw a server balancing a serving tray in one hand. The server said to Meera, "Glad you could make it, finally!"

The huge man stepped aside, pointed to the small group adjacent to the tent. Without smiling, the security man said, "Over there." As Meera walked to the servers, the waitress that had vouched for her winked at her.

Reaching the servers, a man who had some form of supervisor position saw Meera arrive and said, "Next time, could you get here on time? The lockers are behind the tent. Get changed." Meera found the locker area, changed into a server's tuxedo uniform, grabbed a tray of stuffed clams, and wandered into the crowd.

As Meera walked among the elite, she saw the flash of a match outside the security line.

In the seconds where the match was lit, the evil face of a

member of Top-Hat's crew appeared, with an expression of pure hate. Meera then saw the flash of another match, and then another, and then another, and still another. In the flash of each match, there was a different gang-member, each with a unique expression of hatred glaring at Meera through the darkness.

They are out there. Waiting. Meera realized that for the rest of the night, she needed to remain a server at a semi-legal opera performance.

Some time later, as Meera moved through the crowd, she felt a hand clamp on her elbow.

Meera looked and saw the smiling gangster right next to her. Top-Hat hissed, "What makes you think that the Apaches weren't paid to set up this little-get together? We control the docks. The head of security knows me."

Top-Hat grabbed for the back of Meera's neck, the way a cruel man would grab a puppy he was about to throw into a river. Meera, weaponless, slapped the gangster. The crack of her blow against his skin echoed across the dock.

The heads of the celebrants turned, the wealthy guests gasped. A look of shock spread across Top-Hat's face as the gangster realized he wasn't in a back-alley talking to homeless youth with no options, with no witnesses.

Top-Hat had forgotten the first rule of selling danger to the wealthy, that the wealthy guests were at the semi-legal party to briefly experience the illusion of danger, not to see actual crime.

The huge security man glared hatred at Top-Hat. Fear spread over Top-Hat's face. The gangster let go of Meera's arm and disappeared into the crowd.

From the crowd, Ms. Perez-Sanchez walked to Meera and asked, "Can we talk?"

Chapter 17

August Ording had planned to break and rebuild Thadeus Martin using dark occult rituals. The mutated Mr. Martin would be a creature, controlled by Ording, that would control the minds of others. This was how Ording would get his ultimate revenge.

It was 1952 in Madrid. Ording had developed the magic to mutate humans into *die schädel* when he was an officer in the occult special weapons branch of the Axis war machine. Desperate for cash, August Ording planned to recreate the *die schädel* and offer his services to the Apache Crime Family in exchange for passage out of Spain.

Ording tattooed occult sigils and forgotten hieroglyphs on Thadeus Martin. The tattoos bent Thadeus' body and mind. Over the course of days, Ording chanted forgotten and forbidden incantations that channeled mystic powers to stretch Thadeus' body to over six feet, and then further, until the young man was close to seven feet in height.

Thadeus' skin became pale and started to bleach itself. By the end of the ritual, Thadeus' skin had the hue of a porcelain wash basin.

The young man's teeth and hair fell out.

Thadeus' physical changes were manifestations of mental changes. As Thadeus grew taller, he lost most of his ability to communicate. As his hair and teeth fell out, he lost his ability to make independent decisions. Using dark magic, August bound Thadeus' willpower into a magick mirror, stealing the young man's ability to resist.

The occult rituals stole Thadeus' ability to think, but gave the broken man telepathy. When Ording commanded, Thadeus' body would emit a loud buzzing, humming-type sound. While the occult creature hummed, it would glare at the intended victim. If the victim was a young person, a soldier in the prime of life, the *die schädel* would have to look directly into the person's eyes to obtain control. If the victim was older, in poor health, or very young, the *die schädel* could be feet away and seize control of the victim's brain.

The Apaches had provided Ording with a flat in a five-floor walk-up. August Ording lay on the blanket on the box spring that served as a bed, proudly staring at his creation as it sat motionless on a folding chair, when he heard the racket of young men in the building's stairwell.

August guessed it was the Apaches returning to check on their investment. August recognized the voice of Aldi, a low-level Apache. *He's arguing about money,* realized August. *A man in the group is saying Aldi is holding out on them. Aldi is denying it.*

August listened to the group of young men push and shove and jostle each other on the stairs. At night, August returned to hide in Las Descalzas Reales Monastery, but his days were spent with the *die schädel* in the Apache studio. August looked around the flat. *I have spent four days in this dump, working like a dog for these people.*

Soon things will change. A smile crept onto August's face as he planned.

The door to August's flat flung open. In marched four Apaches, the youngest being the barely-out-of-second-ary-school Aldi. The oldest was a young man called Top-Hat. Top-Hat had the nasty expression of someone who had been recently humiliated pasted on his face and was still salty from the experience. The last two Apaches were nearly identical. Short, squat and walked like wrestlers.

As the four marched in, they gave August the same amount of attention a bad housekeeper would give a half-dead houseplant. Aldi was insisting, "Top-Hat, look, the guy is short-changing you. He shorted the payment and now he's lying about it. I can take care of it, but I need time."

As Aldi lectured, he marched over to the pale, toothless, balding *die schädel.* August's creation sat in a folding chair, drooling and staring into space. After a moment of slacked-jawed staring, Aldi asked August, "How is this useless sack of waste going to get us money?"

August was a technical occultist, not a sorcerer. The difference between a technical occultist and sorcerer was like the difference between a short-order line cook in a sandwich shop and a trained chef. The line cook had been trained to do one thing and do it very well. A chef had gone to school for years and could make a gourmet meal out of whatever was lying around the kitchen. August was no chef. August Ording knew how to make the creature *die schädel* and knew a few other spells taught to him for survival. Magick combat, or regular combat, wasn't something the former librarian was capable of.

August started to think and plan. *The leader is obviously Top-Hat. Aldi is the young up-and-comer trying to make as much money and get as rich as possible as quickly as possible.*

The two other gentlemen are average thugs, rough Apaches who do the gang's rough work. Not too bright, not too stupid, not tough enough to make it as boxers, but rougher than the average man.

August thoughts were interrupted when Aldi

demanded, "Uh, Hello? Anyone there? What the heck is this?"

"This creature can make anyone hand over money," said Ording. "Aldi, please stand in front of the creature."

Aldi growled, "Screw you!" and the rough Apaches burst out laughing.

Top-Hat said, "Nah, let's see what Ording's got."

Aldi walked in front of the *die schädel*. August walked to the side of the creature and whispered a command.

Humming came from the *die schädel*. Aldi's eyes rolled back into his eye-sockets.

The rough Apaches took a step back. Top-Hat had no reaction.

August whispered something else to the creature. The creature got up, grabbed Aldi's head, and stared into the young Apache's eyes.

The two rough Apaches glanced at one another, looks of worry on their faces. August could tell they were asking themselves, "Should we do something?" Top-Hat held up a hand in the "stop" gesture, and the rough Apaches stood still.

Aldi was shaking where he stood, trembling as if he would start convulsing. Suddenly, Aldi stopped. The creature let go of the young Apache and sat down. The humming stopped. Aldi stood still for a second, blinked twice, and then turned back to the other Apaches.

Aldi looked at himself, then the others in the room, smiled and said, "That's it? We bought an ugly man who grabs and stares?"

The two rough Apaches burst out laughing and started to advance towards August. It was their job to deliver beatings to people who failed the Apaches, and the rough Apaches were eager to start work.

Top-Hat growled to August, "If there is something else you care to demonstrate, now would be the time."

August said, "Ask about the money."

The rough Apaches stopped mid-stride. Aldi's face burst into a pale version of itself, and the young Apache started to stammer, "Money, money? What about the money? I told you everything I know about . . ."

Top-Hat hissed an interruption, "Tell me the truth."

Aldi started to shake uncontrollably. The muscles of his neck sprang out in strands against the skin, as if he was willing his jaw to stay closed but the mouth seemed to function on its own. Even Aldi's voice was different.

Instead of having a playful cadence to it, as when Aldi answered Top-Hat's question, his voice sounded as if Aldi was shouting his answer from a place very far away.

"I lied!" screeched Aldi. "I lied!! Of course the old man paid! He always pays! He lives in terror of you! I just planned to rip you and him off! I just planned—"

Top-Hat barked another interruption, "You planned

to rip me off?" The Apache leader snapped his fingers to get the attention of the rough Apaches, and then pointed to Aldi.

The two men rushed towards Aldi, who started to scream.

"Shut up," said Top-Hat, and Aldi did so.

As the brutish Apaches dragged Aldi from the room, August wonder if they would kill the young man or just beat him to within inches of his life. August was tempted to ask, but decided not to when Top-Hat said, "Why don't you start explaining what other things this creature can do?"

Chapter 18

Sweaty and out of breath, the CEO of Smithburg Office Supplies pulled into the parking lot across from a small second-hand store. Roland hadn't been in the store in years. Memories from his youth flooded back to him.

It was 1952, Madrid. For years, Roland O'Brien had lived a double-life. There was the facade he showed to the reputable business world, but in reality, Roland was a womanizing thief who defrauded his employer and cheated on his wife. Roland's crimes had started to catch up with him.

The Apaches, the crime organization who helped Roland send an innocent man to prison, had bullied their way into Roland's life. Unable to go to the police for help, fearing Apaches would rat on him for his crimes, Roland was trapped on one side by the Apaches. On the other side was his divorce.

Ms. Perez-Sanchez, the lawyer for his wife, was pushing for an investigation into his finances. How Ms. Perez-Sanchez found out so much about his finances, Roland didn't know, Roland couldn't even keep track of the paperwork in his home office. But Roland knew that with an investigation, it was only a matter of time before his and the Apache's uncontrolled stealing from Smithburg was discovered and everyone would be sent to jail. Roland had to run, to ditch his life in Madrid, to flee to America.

The Apaches have informants at every airport, port, and train station, the thief thought. *I need someone to sneak me to France or England.* Roland's only non-Apache contact who might know about smuggling was a small-time crook he hadn't talked to in years. As Roland opened the door to the thrift store that served as the front for Petey The Fence's criminal activities, Roland prayed that Petey didn't hold a grudge.

Hearing a bell go ring-a-ling as he swung open the store's door and stepped inside. Petey, owner of the store, stood behind a waist-high display case and wore a light sweater. Roland noticed there was only one customer. She was a small and thin Irish girl, the type that got work as a nanny or household help in Spain.

Roland bellowed, "Petey-boy! How you been?"

Petey looked at the young lady and said, "I'll talk to you later, Beliz."

The young lady nodded to Petey, walked past Roland, and left the store.

Petey greeted Roland with a calm, "Roland. It's been some time."

Roland was shocked at the transformation of his friend and the thought forced itself into his mind, *Petey's put on weight! He's been eating good!* Roland tried and failed to control the smirk that forced itself onto his face as he thought, *Or drinking good! Petey always liked the lager!*

Roland blurted out the words, "You're looking well-fed, my friend!" as he let a huge smile spread to his face. He stretched out his right hand to initiate a handshake. Roland also lifted and spread out his left arm to start a hug.

Petey remained behind the second-hand store's glass counter, dashing any chances for a hug. Petey did grab Roland's right hand, gave it two business-like pumps, and asked, "It's been a long time. What can I help you with?"

Roland sputtered, "It's almost like you're not glad to see me."

Petey answered, "I'm not."

Roland decided to cut to the chase and said, "Do you know anyone that can get me out of the country?"

Petey snorted, "Look around the store. Do you see anything you'd like?"

A confused Roland looked around the store, at the half-bare shelves, at the empty customer floor. Realization of Petey's new economic reality set in. *This place should be packed, all the time. Packed!* realized Roland. *Thieves coming in with stolen goods to sell, buyers looking for stuff to buy.*

"What happened?" Roland asked. Petey then removed his sweater and stood in the unshaded light of the store's one bright bulb. Without the sweater and in the light, Roland appreciated the change in his old acquaintance and thought, *Petey's got the rock-hard body of a body-builder . . . or a criminal. A jail-bird who has been in cell-block D and has spent the time lifting.*

Petey growled, "Look at this stinking place. Just look at it. Everything in here is crap." Roland noticed Petey slowly making his way to the store's front door. Roland realized, *I've got to get out of here.*

Petey started to lecture, "You missed big changes. Changes since the last time you were here."

Roland's hands started to shake as he thought, *Oh God.*

Petey's lecture continued, "The place got raided. The network of . . ." Petey's story paused for a moment, as the trader of stolen goods struggled to find the right words to describe the thieves he knew, ". . . suppliers got rounded up and arrested."

Petey reached the front door and locked it. Petey continued, "I got locked up for a year!"

Roland realized Petey the Fence, opportunistic drunk thief, had become Petey the Fence, tough career criminal.

Roland felt the weight of the beer-gut he had developed over the years and was aware of the skinniness of his arms. Like a mind-reader, Petey said, "You used to have arms like tree-trunks. When was the last time you were in the ring?"

Roland stammered, "I didn't know your situation."

Petey answered, "I know yours."

Roland involuntarily swallowed and thought, *Oh no,* and sputtered, "Hey Petey, how's about a drink?"

Petey snapped, "I quit drinking. And you're not smart enough to build a company like the one you're running. How'd you get it?"

Roland said nothing, his mind trying to think of a be-lievable lie to tell Petey.

Petey didn't wait for Roland to think. The criminal growled, "You tell me how you got the business, and I'll tell you my new role in it."

A shocked Roland said nothing. Roland heard Petey growl, "Well? What's the story? I remembered your part-ner. I seen him around the town before he got arrested. An idiot-savant when it came to business. Great with numbers, couldn't get laid to save his life."

Things were pretty good with that skinny little guy, Roland admitted. A small wave of sadness passed through Roland, and the CEO of Smithburg Corporation almost asked himself, *Would things have stayed good if I hadn't wanted more?*

Roland noticed that Petey was staring at him the way a lion stares at a nice, tender antelope.

Petey stated, "I know you're not smart enough to run a business. I know that the only reason you're here is because you've run that Smithburg into the ground."

Roland nervously thought, *How much money does this guy want? What is he going to do if I don't come up with the cash?*

Petey stated, "I can run a business. I make this place run, even though conditions are terrible."

Roland started to shake as he realized what Petey wanted.

Petey stated, "Hire me as a consultant for Smithburg. I'll turn that place around."

Roland realized the true meaning behind Petey's words and thought, *He's taking over Smithburg the same way I took over Smithburg.*

Not showing any emotion, Roland thought, *Let him take over. Promise him the company, let him go down with the Apaches.* He said, "That's a great idea. I just need help dealing with my divorce first."

CHAPTER 19

Roland knew Pete "The Fence" Kolems had been out of prison less than a year. Roland knew Pete Kolems was desperate for cash. Roland knew Pete Kolems could kill a man and disappear into the criminal underworld. Roland thought, *I hope this plan works out. If that bitch takes all my money, I'm going to be reduced to busing tables in Latvia.*

It was 1952, in Madrid, Spain. Pete "Petey The Fence" Kolems was driving Roland O'Brien to meet Roxanne O'Brien's divorce lawyer. Both Pete and Roland wondered how much Ms. Perez-Sanchez knew about Roland's thievery.

"I just have to survive the legal shellacking of my divorce," Roland told Petey. "After the divorce, I'll hire you as co-CEO of Smithburg. When you're co-CEO, you'll get me out of Spain, I'll disappear in America, and everything is yours." Roland had left out the fact that the Apache Crime Family had riddled the company with thieves, and that Spain's moral police would probably start an investigation into the company.

Hearing Roland's offer, Petey nodded his head and said, "Sounds good."

As Roland O'Brien and Peter Kolems drove to the meeting, Ms. Perez-Sanchez enjoyed the view from her law office on the penthouse floor of the exclusive Metropolis Building. As the lawyer relaxed in the cool air of the recently installed American air-conditioning system, Ms. Perez-Sanchez pictured Roland O'Brien whimpering for legal mercy.

Ms. Perez-Sanchez loved her job, her profession, and her life. The lawyer, whom a bitter male adversary once described as a "pissed-off dragon with a law degree," often described herself to female law students as "a crusader for proper treatment."

Ms. Perez-Sanchez didn't use the term "crusader" as hyperbole. After her first disastrous teenage marriage ended horribly, Ms. Perez-Sanchez found a passion for legal revenge. The young Perez-Sanchez went back to school, finished secondary school, university, and then law school. Since law school, Ms. Perez-Sanchez used her law degree as a sword against twisted justice.

Fifteen years after her first husband stole all their marriage's money and moved in with another woman, Ms. Perez-Sanchez sued him. Knowing that she would never win a divorce case, because divorce didn't exist in 1950s Spain, Ms. Perez-Sanchez sued for fraud. Ms. Perez-Sanchez testified in court that her ex-husband had insisted he was an employed, licensed mechanic who was able to support a family of three. "He swore up and down that he was a good handyman, that he knew what he was doing, even in the bedroom," Ms. Perez-Sanchez testified, her phrasing drawing a gasp of shock from the 1950s conservative crowd, "but on our wedding night, he couldn't even get the Sears & Roebuck bedroom set assembled."

Ms. Perez-Sanchez's mild dig at her husband caused laughs in the courtroom, won over the jury, got her a huge settlement, and helped Perez-Sanchez find her true calling. In the years since her legal punishment of her husband, the charismatic lawyer had helped woman after woman get more than acceptable settlements, even when the husband was a tricky bastard.

Ms. Perez-Sanchez smiled as she recalled, *Getting a divorce in England and then having it recognized here in Spain was an inspiration from God.*

The retired flyweight boxer Paul Kanie knocked on Ms. Perez-Sanchez's office door. Ms. Perez-Sanchez called,

"Come in!"

Sticking his head into her office, Mr. Kanie announced, "Miss? The latest adversaries have arrived."

Ms. Perez-Sanchez smiled, got up from her desk, and was escorted by Mr. Kanie to the office reception area.

As Ms. Perez-Sanchez watched Mr. O'Brien stomp into her office, followed by Petey in his ill-fitting suit, the skilled lawyer slipped a note to her receptionist. The note said, "A peseta says Roland is the type of man who freaks out."

Ms. Perez-Sanchez's receptionist snickered and said, "No bet."

Pete the Fence noticed the snicker between the dragon lawyer and the receptionist. Hiding his rage at the laughter he knew was directed at him, Peter started to look at the law office of Perez-Sanchez the way a jewel thief looked at a Cartier window.

Peter's casing of the office was deeply disappointing. In making Roland a victim, Peter had a buffet of flaws to exploit in wreaking Roland's life. *Roland's a greedy bastard,* thought the criminal, *and proud to the point of insanity, too proud to go to the cops and rat on me. If Roland went to the cops, he'd have to confess all the stupid things he's done.*

Seeing the confident stride of the women who populated Ms. Perez-Sanchez office, Petey The Fence thought, *There's nothing here! There's not a gosh darn thing here! There's not a gosh darn thing here that I can use!*

I need someone, Peter the Fence thought. *I need someone on the inside, someone to tell me what Perez-Sanchez's vices are. Does she have a young lover? A stud that she is cheating on her husband with? This office costs money, maybe she's over extended her credit.*

Peter began to worry. The terrible thought that he may actually lose to a woman started to form in his mind. That's when Peter recognized Paul Kanie.

Confidence surged in Peter. Peter haunted the dozens of run-down boxing gyms in Madrid and had a passing acquaintance with the ex-flyweight. Seeing Paul hold the door open to the conference room Roland and Peter were being led to, Peter thought, *That's it. That's my in.*

Peter remembered all the drivers and doormen he had known over the years, all the men that smiled as the wives of the rich husbands, all the hiding resentment in the men that held those jobs. *I didn't know things were so bad Paul had to take a job working for a woman,* thought Peter, *but this will work to my advantage.*

Entering the conference room behind Roland, Peter gave Paul's elbow a soft squeeze as the two passed. Paul returned a barely noticeable nod in recognition. Peter felt a confident excitement run though him as he thought, *The fix. The fix is in the bag.*

Peter sat in the conference room, the sun shining in through the windows behind him, staring out the windows on the opposite side of the room that gave a view of the beige hall outside of Ms. Perez-Sanchez office, the view allowed Peter to keep an eye on the wanderings of Paul Kanie. Peter barely paid attention to what the lawyer and her assistants spoke about, expressing annoyance at the soft drinks he was occasionally offered. Everything else Peter did, he did to passively show that he was above everything that happened in the room.

The only time Peter felt comfortable at all was when Roland showed some guts and snarled at Ms. Perez-Sanchez. "You've been lecturing me on and on about what I have to do for over an hour. How about what my wife has to do? Can we get to that?"

Ms. Perez-Sanchez expertly annoyed Roland by not answering his question, by ignoring him for just a few seconds more than was comfortable, by looking at what appeared to be a blank piece of paper for more than a few seconds. Ms. Perez-Sanchez must have heard, or somehow felt, Roland take a deep breath—the type of breath that an angry man takes before bellowing a command.

A half-second before Mr. O'Brien raged his words, Ms. Perez-Sanchez turned to Roland and very sweetly said, "What was that? You said something?" Ms. Perez-Sanchez's cool dismissal of Roland caused the out-thought CEO to hiss, "This is a pain in the ass! All this is a pain in the ass! You're a pain in the—" Roland stopped himself from continuing, when he saw the feigned shocked expression on Ms. Perez-Sanchez's face.

Even Roland could see the fakeness in Ms. Perez-Sanchez's expression. On cue, one of the assistants gasped in faux-horror and another exclaimed, "This! This is verbal abuse! The judge will hear about this!"

Roland's face turned red with fury, and the Smithburg CEO started to stutter a curse. Peter thought, *She has us. We haven't even been in front of a judge yet, and Ms. Perez-Sanchez has beat us. The lady lawyer has three witnesses that can swear Roland can't control his temper. Any judge will side with Roland's wife, saying Roland is abusive.*

Peter stepped between Roland and the Perez-Sanchez team. With a hand on Roland's chest, the Fence said the words, "Could we grab a smoke?" as he thought, *Think this out. I've got to think this out.*

Ms. Perez-Sanchez answered Peter, "Please do. I feel Roland needs to compose himself."

On the way to the men's room, Pete caught the eye of Paul Kanie and mouthed the word, "Smoke?"

Paul followed Roland and Peter into the bathroom. After checking to see that there was no one in the stalls, Peter lit up a cigarette, turned to Paul the Boxer and said, "Paul! Buddy! How you been?"

Paul replied, "I'm good. Surprise to see you here." There was something in Paul's voice, a calmness and coldness, that Petey The Fence wasn't happy to hear.

Struggling to understand why Paul was hiding his rage, Peter asked, "What's it like working for that bitch?" Peter waited for Paul to spew venom, for Paul to piss out words like "nightmare" or "whore."

Paul calmly said, "I wouldn't know. I work for a lady that pays on time and doesn't work me too hard."

Petey The Fence lost his temper. Swingingly widely, Peter pounced toward Paul the Boxer.

An explosion of pain erupted in Peter's midsection, and the professional boxer landed a single perfect upper-cut to the criminal's breadbasket. Peter crumpled to the floor. Paul growled, "I got a good racket going here. Open a few doors, chase away a few rummies. Pay's more steady than anything I ever made in the ring."

As Peter struggled to get up from the floor, Paul said, "I know the way you operate. I don't want none of it. From now on, you don't know me." Paul left the bathroom.

Roland stared at Petey The Fence. As Peter struggled to get up off his knees, Roland thought, *Jesus. I hope this bastard doesn't take this downturn out on me.* Peter succeeded in getting up off the floor.

Turning to Roland, Peter growled, "Roland, we may have a problem. You better call your lawyers."

CHAPTER 20

Top-Hat, dressed in the black attire and white collar of a catholic priest, smiled as he grabbed the thick roll of pesetas from the hands of the middle-aged matron. Stuffing the money into a burlap bag, the criminal thought, *This is the best scam I have ever been part of.*

It was 1952 in Madrid, Spain. To escape the Caudillo of Spain, the occult fugitive August Ording had struck a deal with the Apache Crime Family. The spell-caster had promised the Apaches an occult device that would generate thousands in cash. After seeing the living occult weapon called the *die schädel*, Top-Hat muttered, "If we set something up in Salamanca, we might get something that would generate real money."

Salamanca was a challenging neighborhood to run a scam. The wealthiest section of Madrid, Salamanca was dotted with churches on every other block. In front of every church was a plaza. After the war, hustlers flooded the Salamanca plazas. The various scam-artists claimed to be priests, monks, or brothers collecting money to help those impacted by the war.

To cure Salamanca of crime, Dictator Franco rounded up everyone wearing a religious smock on the plazas. All the holy people the Archbishop of Madrid didn't recognize were taken to the edge of the Manzanares river, had their hands and feet tied, and shoved into the rushing waters. Caudillo Franco's reasoning was, "If they are truly servants of God, The Lord will miracle them to the other side." The Caudillo's brutal method wiped out the con-artist problem.

In the years since Franco's Baptism, the Plazas had become the gathering places of the wealthy grandmothers and widows who attended the churches of the Salamanca district. Top-Hat convinced three of his most-innocent looking female pickpockets to dress as members of The Order Of The Most Holy Sisters Of The Godly Faith and give leaflets to the older women—leaflets stating there would be a meeting to raise money for a mission.

The fake nuns had the effect Top-Hat wanted. A buzz was created among the older, bored church-going women. When Top-Hat opened the front door to the storefront church where the fake nuns had advertised the fund-raiser was being held, there was already a line of people stretching half-way down the block.

As Top-Hat looked at the line of widows and house-wives, all of which were with their mother or married to a man that had pull with Dictator Franco, Top-Hat realized, *If the die schädel doesn't convince the ladies that this is legit, I am going to be very wet for a very short time.*

Top-Hat opened the door and led the first group of ladies into the room where the criminals had the *die schädel*. The *die schädel* sat in his seat, looking barely alive, dressed as a monk, sitting in a large-straight backed wooden chair, in front of the room's bay window. Top-Hat looked at the *die schädel* and a wave of fear rushed into him as he thought, *That pale, drooling freak won't fool anyone! What made me think this was a good idea?*

On the *die schädel's* right stood August Ording, dressed in the black clothing of a priest. On the creature's left was a small cabinet with a bowl of water and an empty glass. In front of the *die schädel* were three rows of folding chairs, twelve seats to a row. Between the chairs and the *die schädel*, there was barely any room to move in the cramped space. In their corner of the room there was a small, portable, stand-alone folding privacy screen, the kind made of wood panels. Behind the panels, Top-Hat had thrown his and Ording's street clothes.

A gasp escaped from the ladies as they entered the flat. They were stunned at the pale thing, sitting with his back to the room's bay window. Top-Hat realized, *These ladies come to these missions for adventure. They expected the movie star Stewart Granger.* Top-Hat heard the murmurs of doubt among the ladies. As the ladies found seats in the chairs facing the *die schädel,* Top-Hat realized he would have to start his sales pitch if he was going to see any money at all.

Top-Hat waved his hand in the direction of the *die schädel* and said, "Ladies, this is the most holy Reverend Karol Józef. He had just returned from the dangerous badlands near Russia. What the Rev. Józef has seen in his travels threatens the existence of our civilization to its core!"

Top-Hat heard the ladies gasp again, but this time the gasp had just a touch of surprised excitement instead of disappointment. *The ladies like stories of dangerous badlands.*

Top-Hat continued, "It's true. You've all heard the rumors of the Kannakannack Valley. The valley that grows the weed straight from the rings of hell. The weed that, when smoked once by a good Christian, transforms the God-fearing man into a lazy, weed-smoking bastard who cares about nothing!"

Top-Hat heard another gasp from a larger section of the audience.

"The weed that changes a man from a productive member of society to a drunken bum, a cheater, a spend-thrift, a man who wastes his life in the company of the dregs of society."

Top-Hat heard a woman in the crowd whisper to her friend, "How did that sick looking man even get around?"

Top-Hat continued, "The Reverend's devotion to the Lord's Word has taken a toll on his health. After a bout with Lassa Fever, the Reverend returned to Spain to raise money to continue his mission."

Top-Hat heard another series of "Oh!" from the crowd. Sensing the ladies were all paying attention, Top-Hat moved to stand behind the *die schädel,* and gave a very slight nod to Ording. Ording had promised Top-Hat that the creature's spell would not affect the gangster.

Ording squeezed the *die schädel's* shoulder. The *die schädel* started to hum.

As the humming permeated the skins and bodies of the women, their eyes rolled back into their sockets, their mouths dropped open. Ording whispered to Top-Hat, "Now they are in the trance."

Top-Hat swallowed hard, nervous, unsure how loud to speak. The criminal whispered, "Get the money." Ording squeezed the *die schädel's* shoulder a second time, a signal to continue.

A guttural, choking sound came from the *die schädel.* A sound that could have been words if the creature was more human.

The ladies reached into their bags and purses, holding all the cash they had on them. Top-Hat quickly went to the cabinet next to the *die schädel*, opened the cabinet's door, and took out a burlap sack.

Top-Hat went from lady to lady, grabbing the money, stuffing the cash into the burlap bag. In less than a minute, Top-Hat had grabbed all the money the ladies had held.

Top-Hat stuffed the burlap sack back into its hiding place and took a few deep breaths to calm himself.

I'm not out of the woods yet, thought the criminal, and then pointed to Ording a third time.

Ording squeezed the *die schädel's* shoulder a third time.

The *die schädel* hissed another series of strange sounds. The ladies put away their bags and purses.

Top-Hat licked his lips and felt the tension in his body relax, and the thought popped into his mind, *This is going to work. I am going to get away with it.*

Top-Hat nodded to Ording, giving him the final signal. Ording snapped his fingers, and the ladies in the room started to blink and come out of the trance they were in. They started to excitedly talk among themselves, telling each other, "What a great speaker the Reverend is! So pious!"

Ording knew, and Top-Hat suspected, that the ladies would stop believing what they were saying in a few weeks or days. Top-Hat knew that if the ladies stopped believing the *die schädel* was the reverend something-or-other in a few days, it didn't matter. The Apaches would have packed up and been long gone, waiting to pull the scam again next year, when the memories of the ladies had faded and the group was eager for a touch of adventure again.

At the end of the day, when the canvas bag was stuffed with cash and Franco's Social Investigation Brigade hadn't knocked down the doors, Top-Hat breathed a sigh of relief. Relaxation spread through the criminal.

As the Apaches counted their money, Top-Hat praised Ording. "My friend, if this keeps up, we will be very wealthy men."

Ording replied, "As long as I make enough to get to California, I'll be happy."

Top-Hat thought, *If we keep making money, I'll never let you get to California. This set-up is too good to let go.*

CHAPTER 21

THE APACHE'S ROBBING OF INNOCENTS MIGHT HAVE CONtinued for years, but four unrelated events occurred within minutes of one another that had dire consequences for the criminals.

The first event was when Beliz Kelly, a domestic who worked for Ms. Perez-Sanchez, inadvertently betrayed Roxanne O'Brien.

It was 1952, Madrid. Ms. Perez-Sanchez was enjoying an afternoon game of Tute with her newest bodyguard, Meera the Sardincian, and The Sisters.

The Sisters were a small group of wealthy women who realized not all divorced men accepted their divorces properly. The Sisters let soon-to-be divorced women stay at a series of villas until the ex-husbands accepted their new reality.

Beliz had just brought the table a fresh carafe of Sangria when one of the Sisters asked Ms. Perez-Sanchez, "And the new girl, Roxanne? Where is she right now?"

Ms. Perez-Sanchez replied, "32 Milla de Oro," which was one of the dozens of secret locations where friends of the Sisters stayed.

The Sister replied, "Excellent!" then asked, "Meera, have you been to #32?"

Meera answered, "Yes, it's beautiful," and then thanked Beliz, the petite girl pouring the Sangria.

Beliz showed no emotion at hearing the address. But inside Beliz, excitement raced.

Milla de Oro, thought the young woman, *the street of Gold. The richest, most exclusive street in all of Madrid.*

Growing up in Leitrim, by far the poorest of the counties in Ireland, the young girl had always dreamed of wealth. After moving to Spain, the barely out of her teens young woman realized wealth didn't grow on trees and that she would be serving drinks to old ladies until she was a senior citizen.

Trying to drown her sorrows in drink at Micheal's bar, Beliz drunkenly complained to her boyfriend, "32 Milla de Oro! That divorced bitch is staying at some mansion while I am serving drinks! The church doesn't even allow divorce! It's a sin!"

Aldi, the part-time bartender and full-time Apache, didn't really understand what the Irish girl was complaining about. But the criminal did understand enough English to know 'divorced' meant 'divorciada' and 'thirty-two Milla de Oro' meant 'treinta y dos Milla de Oro.' The tricky gangster knew Top-Hat would pay good money for information when The Sisters hid their friends.

The second event that led to the end of the Apaches robbing widows was the strong-arming of Pete Kolems.

Pete Kolems stood behind the counter at his empty second hand-store, knowing his scam with Roland O'Brien was going down the tubes as quickly as it had gone up the tubes, when three Apaches walked in.

The first Apache announced, "Peter, my man, have we got a deal for you!"

A second Apache picked up a blender that sat on the store counter and smashed the blender into a dozen pieces. The Apache announced, "Petey-O, you don't have any inventory. Your stuff keeps breaking! You want our stuff because you need our stuff!" The third Apache put a shipping cardboard box on the store's counter.

Realizing he had no choice, Peter pulled back a box flap. The box was filled to the brim with staplers, staples, staple removers, binders, and hole-punchers.

"Office supplies?" Peter said. "Office supplies? What,

you guys knock over an office supply warehouse? The streets are covered with hole-punchers these days." Peter stopped himself from talking any further, as a realization came to him.

Peter picked up a hole-puncher, turned it over, and saw, "A Smithburg Office Supply Product."

Peter realized, *It's not Roland who's doing the robbing. It's Roland who's getting robbed.* Peter whispered to the Apache, "Hey, buddy, maybe we can make a deal," and a deal was made.

The third event that led to the end of the Apaches robbing widows was when Stephon García stared through the glass kitchen door and heard his mother command, "Stephon, get away from the door!"

There was a tension in Roxanne O'Brien's voice when she called to Stephon that normally was never there. Stephon, barely out of his toddler years, recognized the tension, but didn't understand why the tension was there.

Stephon wanted to know why he couldn't go outside and play in the backyard of #32 Milla de Oro. The little boy refused to move away from the door and pretended that he hadn't heard his mother.

Roxanne walked over to Stephon, stood next to the boy with her arms folded, and commanded, "Stephon, get away from the door."

The boy asked, "Why?" as he continued to stare out the

window.

Roxanne used her willpower not to scream, "Because we are so close to being free of your step-father that I don't want to jinx things by being seen!" and instead said, "Because today is a play-inside day, OK?"

The boy whined, "Every day is a play-inside day."

Roxanne bent down and hugged her son and whispered, "I know, but it's just for a little while longer, OK? Go to your room now, OK?"

Stephon said, "OK."

But Roxanne could tell her little boy was thinking, *Outside. Soon I will be outside.*

Roxanne called out, "Paul?"

Paul, Roxanne's temporary bodyguard, answered from the kitchen, "Yes?"

Roxanne said, "I want you outside. Guarding the backyard."

The fourth event that led to the end of the Apaches robbing widows was the end of Berhtram Braun's investigation into August Ording's whereabouts.

Since his betrayal of August Ording to Spain's Social Investigation Brigade, Berhtram had been locked in the Presidential suite of the Palacio Del Retiro Hotel. Two S.I.B. agents guarded the Presidential suite's door, making sure the Berhtram never left the suite until his job was completed.

Berhtram's job was to identify August Ording. Berhtram sat in the living area of the suite, surrounded by boxes and boxes of passport photos in I.D. cards. It had been years since Berhtram had seen Ording, but after scouring the travel records, the ex-Axis had identified Ording. Bertram had just circled Ording's name in red on the Social Investigation Brigade's I.D. card.

Berhtram leaned back on the overstuffed couch, lit a cigarette, enjoyed the view from his penthouse balcony window, and smiled. "How much money?" Berhtram murmured to himself. "How much money will the Kingdom of Spain give me for this public service? Enough to enjoy years of leisure?"

As Berhtram relaxed, he let happiness and contentment flow over him. At that moment, he heard a faint humming. Berhtram asked himself, "Is that a radio?" But then realization of his situation washed into Berhtram and he croaked, "No. Oh no."

The humming increased, and Berhtram realized he couldn't move. Berhtram tried to scream. The only noise that came from Berhtram was a soft gargling.

The door to the water closet opened. The creature crawled like a spider over to the shaking Berhtram, sat on the edge of the couch, grabbed Berhtram by both sides of his head, and stared into the S.I.B. informant's eyes.

Inside the mind of Berhtram Braun, every horror the

man had ever felt started to replay itself. In one second, Berhtram was his eight-year-old self, running down the street in Bonn. In real life, Berhtram had escaped the crowd of bullies, but in the *die schädel* caused memory, young Berhtram was caught.

After the beating, Berhtram found himself as a teen-ager in his then-girlfriend's room. Abigail's father flung open the door to the bedroom and bellowed, "What are you doing with my daughter?" Even worse than the beating from the girl's father was the stinging words of the girl to her dad, "Daddy! I would never, not with a boy like him!"

Next, Berhtram found himself as an adult on the battle-field of El Alamein. As Berhtram ran from the fighting, he heard the whistle of a bomb approach. Berhtram knew he wouldn't outrun the bomb.

As the perverted and twisted memories played inside Berhtram's mind, he collapsed into a shaking mess on the floor. Hours later, Mr. Brett would find Berhtram in a state useless for anything except a stay in a sanatorium.

The *die schädel* left the way it came, through the bath-room window, crawling down the building wall, unseen in the alleyway between the Palacio Del Retiro Hotel and the hotel next door.

Reaching the alley, the creature crawled into the back seat of the Renault driven by August Ording. Ording pulled a blanket over the creature and said, "I finally figured out what type of murder you are good at. The sneaky kind." Ording threw a cigarette butt, the cigarette butt smoked by Berhtram years earlier, the butt Ording used in his magick ritual to find the informant, out the Renault window.

When Ording arrived back at the flat with the *die schädel*, the Apache guard for the *die schädel* was in a trance, staring at the floor, unmoving. Ording took the key from the comatose gangster, opened the flat door, and whistled for the *die schädel* to get inside.

Ording closed the door, threw the keys on the Apache's lap, and waited for Top-Hat to collect the creature and himself for the afternoon session of robbing widows. As Ording closed his eyes, satisfied with the day's work of personal revenge, he said to himself, "Soon it will be time to head for California."

Shock raged through Ording when he heard Top-Hat, hidden behind the folding curtain, ask, "Why do you think you're going to California?"

CHAPTER 22

August Ording regained consciousness and opened his eyes. Top-Hat, a ranking member of the Apache Crime Family, smiled into the face of the captive spell-weaver and said, "You thought you were pretty clever, trying to betray the Apaches?"

It was 1952 in Madrid. Ording, a spell-caster desperate for cash, had re-created a living occult weapon called the *die schädel* for the Apache Crime Family. The crime family successfully used the hypnotic creature to rob dozens of people and treated the occultist as family.

Ording betrayed the crime family's trust. The spell-caster took the *die schädel* and incapacitated a government informant. Hurting a government agent was a very bad idea. If the Ruler of Spain ever caught on that an Apache associate hurt something that the government wanted safe, there would be terrible repercussions.

Top-Hat had caught Ording in the act of misusing the occult weapon, albeit too late to save the government informant.

Ording woke up tied to a chair in the same fifth-floor flat where the Apaches kept the *die schädel*, and thought, *This is bad.*

As his vision cleared, Ording looked around the room. The *die schädel* sat on its chair, exhausted and pale. Top-Hat stood glaring down at Ording.

Top-Hat was stripped down to his undershirt, stretching his arms and chest, looking like a runner preparing to start a race or a boxer warming up to hit the heavy bag.

Ording glanced to the side of Top-Hat and saw two low-level Apaches standing beside the gangster.

Ording asked, "What are you clowns going to do? Have a go at some calisthenics? Get a few push-ups in?"

Top-Hat pulled a pair of training gloves from his back pocket. The gloves were the type of leather gloves boxers wear for heavy bag training, designed to protect the wearer's hands.

Ording realized, *There's no heavy bag in this room.*

Top-Hat adjusted the gloves, pulled them tight, hit a clenched fist into the palm of the other hand. Top-Hat took a step close to Ording and said, "We should begin."

The two Apaches that had cleared the room marched towards Ording. Ording decided not to wait for what was coming and hissed the command, "eureun aranjeunna!" The *die schädel* snapped up straight and started to hum.

Top-Hat and the Apache soldiers froze. Unable to prevent himself from gloating, Ording hissed at Top-Hat, "Ha. Didn't know I could do that, did you?" Seeing the strain on Top-Hat, Ording added, "I've been working with the creature. Training it. Don't have to squeeze its shoulder anymore. I can verbally command it."

A smile broke out over Ording's face as he glared at Top-Hat and said, "Looks like I won't be getting beaten today."

Ording's face fell open in astonishment when he heard Top-Hat say, "I think the beating is going to happen."

Ording felt despair creep into every cell of his body as he watched the gangster stop pretending to strain against the *die schädel's* powers and pull the collar of his undershirt to the right, just enough to show the Kemet hieroglyph tattoo on his chest. The same mystic design all of Ording's Axis commanders had inked on their body.

Top-Hat said, "You think you were the first Axis to come crawling into Madrid and Paris after the defeat? There were dozens! Dozens of loyal Axis soldiers who were more than willing to give up the secrets they had pledged to take to their graves. They gave up the secret to their occult protection for safe passage to Brazil."

Top-Hat strolled over the room's bay window. Nonchalantly, the gangster asked, "If a man fell from this window, August, how injured do you think he would be? Or would he just die?"

Ording said, "What about the monastery? They are going to miss me!"

Top-Hat replied, "The Church will learn to live without you. The Church of Rome did fine for hundreds of years before you showed up. It will survive you going missing."

Ording knew Top-Hat was right. August's superior in the monastery had suspected that Ording was a fake and would blame Ording's disappearance on a con-artist splitting for New York. The monastery would leave Ording's room in Las Descalzas Reales alone for a few weeks and then give Ording's few possessions to the needy. After the dispersion of his few belongings, any memory of August Ording would fade from memory.

Ording started to mutter excuses about why the Apaches should keep him around. "You, you still need me. The creature won't respond to the commands if I don't give them."

Top-Hat took a step closer to Ording and said, "I'm confident a fall from this height would be just enough to injure a fake priest. Not kill. But enough to injury a man so he doesn't get too smart every again."

In a desperate panic, Ording blurted, "One hypnotizing thief in Madrid is good, but two hypnotizing thieves are better."

Top-Hat stopped walking and asked, "What?"

Ording continued, "One creature in Madrid, one in London. Three hypnotizing thieves would be amazing."

Top-Hat stopped walking and commanded, "Shut up the humming."

Ording murmured, "tulungan abdi."

The creature stopped humming and its body went slack. The Apache goons started to blink, move, and look at each other with dumbfounded expressions.

Top-Hat glared at the goons and said, "Why don't you two idiots wait downstairs?" The enforcers shuffled out of the room.

Top-Hat continued, "An army of creatures. I like that."

Momentarily safe, Ording realized what he had promised and thought, *Can I even do that? How could they be controlled?* Stalling for time, Ording pointed out, "I need men. Men to turn into—"

Top-Hat interrupted, "How about the two useless idiots you had just frozen?"

Ording swallowed hard with the realization that Top-Hat was going to keep him to his promised, make him build an army—an Army of *die schädel.*

Then Ording realized, *Why not?*

The occultist whispered, "I need the *Jomhuri-ye Eslâmi-ye.*"

Top-Hat demanded, "The what?"

Ording whispered, "The *Jomhuri-ye Eslâmi-ye* amulet. I'll need the *Jomhuri-ye Eslâmi-ye* to make a spell of that size work. It was in the British Museum. The Royal Museum was a little hard to get to when I was working for the Axis. Some clown was supposed to steal it and bring it to our side, but that never happened. Guess it got lost in transit."

Top-Hat answered, "Well, I'll see what I can do."

Ording hid his smile and thought, *If that stupid amulet is anywhere in Europe, Top-Hat is going to find it.*

CHAPTER 23

A~LDI~ LISTENED TO R~OLAND~ O'B~RIEN~ WHINE. W~HEN THE~ corrupt businessman muttered the phrase, "She has my talisman! The talisman doesn't belong to her!" Aldi knew he would soon be back in the Apache Crime Family's good graces.

It was 1952 in Madrid, Spain. Hours earlier, the Apache Lieutenant Top-Hat had sent out the message to every Apache member in Europe: "Somewhere there is a missing magical amulet called the *Jomhuri-ye Eslâmi-ye*. Find that thing!"

All over the city, low-level criminals were knocking over pawn-shops and thrift-stores looking for the Persian charm. Pickpockets and sneak-thieves were visiting family they hadn't seen since the holidays, hoping an old aunt or uncle had thrown a worthless keepsake into a kitchen drawer or shoe box—and that the forgotten keepsake was the missing *Jomhuri-ye Eslâmi-ye* Amulet.

Aldi was the lowest of the low in the criminal underworld, a criminal with no active scam or prospect. The Apaches had assigned the delinquent to keep an eye on drunks who the crime family were currently fleecing, to make sure the marks didn't get any ideas.

All day, every day, Aldi spent his time with broken, drinking men who were indebted to the Apaches.

Mimosas at nine am with gambling addicts at the track. The men already in debt to the Apaches would beg Aldi for another loan as they gave him an envelope full of cash to give to Top-Hat.

Sangrias at noon with businessmen whose businesses had failed, but they were too stubborn to admit defeat. Businessmen who begged for another loan at sky-high interest, a loan Aldi would OK, knowing that Apaches would be seizing the businessman's home and car when reality set in.

Pints in the evening with Roland was the baby-sitting job Aldi hated the most.

It's his constant whining, Aldi told himself. *His constant whining is what is driving me nuts.*

Since the start of his divorce, Roland had stopped

showing up for work at Smithburg Office Supplies. The businessman usually slept late, trying to sleep off the hangover from the night before.

Roland usually woke up to the banging of Apaches on his front door, who wanted him to sign and OK a stack of fake invoices they would take to the Smithburg and demand payment for.

Roland, sick of the Apaches, would seek solace with his only friend—Petey The Fence. Petey would let Roland bum around his thrift store as both tried to figure out how to hide money from Roland's soon to be ex-wife.

At five, Roland would head to Micheal's bar for a drink. Most times, Roland would drink with Petey the Fence and Jacques Proust. Aldi loved when the three drank and kept to themselves. Aldi often found it amusing when Petey and Jacques would argue, with Petey accusing Jacques of being an elitist.

Sometimes, Roland drank by himself. During this time, it was Aldi's job was to make sure Roland didn't get drunk and go to the cops.

Aldi, as he served drinks at the bar, heard Roland mutter, "Even my talisman. The wench got her hands on my talisman."

Aldi asked, "Your wife has a talisman?"

Roland continued, "My lawyers are looking for missing financials, and when I heard paperwork was missing, I realized I hadn't seen my amulet in forever. I am guessing the ex-wife nicked it when she nicked the paperwork."

"I don't even think she knows the British Museum would pay to get it back! I keep telling that lawyer of hers that I want my 'paperweight' back because it has sentimental value. Thing looks worthless, so hopefully they won't figure out what it is and they'll give it to me."

Aldi said nothing. The gangster just planned.

Aldi called Top-Hat to deliver the message, "Roxanne O'Brien has a talisman from the British Museum. You may want to check it out."

CHAPTER 24

THE GANGSTER TOP-HAT BELIEVED ROXANNE O'BRIEN had the *Jomhuri-ye Eslâmi-ye* Talisman hidden somewhere. The gangster was willing to use viciousness and the living occult weapon called the *die schädel* to get the magick amulet.

It was 1952, Madrid. Top-Hat sat behind the driver's wheel of a Renault parked in front of #32 Milla de Oro. In the backseat sat the fugitive August Ording, a fugitive occultist willing to do anything to be smuggled to California. Next to Ording, wrapped in a dark hijab so that only his eyes showed, was the occult creature *die schädel*.

Milla de Oro Avenue was home to the wealthy captains of industry who kept Dictator Franco in power. In return,

Dictator Franco commanded the Mayor of Madrid to use all means necessary to keep the industrialists living on Milla de Oro safe from the crime plaguing the rest of Spain.

Mayor José installed a police cabana at either end of the wealthy avenue. The small booths resembled an enclosed bus kiosk and were manned twenty-four hours a day with two Metro officers each. These four officers were tasked with keeping the playground of the wealthy quiet and safe.

Top-Hat looked up and down Milla de Oro and saw the street was deserted. The residents of the street, like the rest of Spain, were enjoying the afternoon siesta.

Top-Hat stared over the driving wheel of the car and decided it was time to act. Top-Hat stated, "Roxanne has a kid."

The color drained from Ording's face. His frustrated expression was replaced with a look of shock. Somehow, Ording managed to whisper the word, "So?"

Top-Hat said, "Once we get her kid, Roxanne will bring us whatever we want."

Ording didn't move.

Top-Hat flatly stated, "No kid, no ticket to L.A."

A look of resignation spread across Ording's face. He reached across the back-seat of the Renault and squeezed the *die schädel's* shoulder.

Inside the kiosk, yards away from the parked car, only one of the four officers was awake. The day had been uneventful, so the group of cops decided to get a cat-nap in. The officer that was awake stared at the Renault parked on the avenue. As the officer stared at the car, he felt his eyes-lids grow heavy, and he felt a tiredness he couldn't resist. In seconds, the officer was in a trance-like state, and appeared to sleep standing up.

Inside the Renault, Ording had his hand on the humming creature. Like a skilled animal trainer, Ording could sense what the creature could accomplish. The occultist blurted out, "The cops are asleep. In a light sleep."

Top-Hat growled, "Make whoever is in the house sleep."

Ording squeezed the shoulder of the *die schädel* again. The humming of the creature changed slightly.

Inside #32 Milla de Oro, Roxanne sighed. Her light sleep became much deeper and developed into a coma-like trance. Next to Roxanne, her son, Stephon García, lay quiet.

Top-Hat growled, "Get him."

Ording squeezed the shoulder of the creature and whispered, "Get the boy."

Ording popped open the door of the car. The creature quickly crawled out of the car, its arms slapping on the sidewalk as it moved with its belly hugging the ground.

From the kiosk, in his state of near somnambulism, the watching officer remarked, "What a large, odd spider."

The creature crawled across the ground until it reached the ten-foot wrought-iron fence that surrounded #32 Milla

De Oro. The creature grabbed the bars of the fence, felt how solid the iron was, and let go.

The creature, like a confused dog, looked back at the Renault. Like an animal trainer frustrated that its charge didn't perform better, Ording hissed at the *die schädel*, "Go! Go!"

The creature turned back to the bars and scuttled along the edge of the fence. Reaching the gate, the creature looked up and saw the simple handle that kept the gate closed.

From the car, Ording encouraged, "Go on, do it, do it!"

The creature reached up and pawed at the handle, the way a dog might paw at a device it didn't understand but saw its master use. The creature successfully pawed the handle up, unlocking the gate. The gate opened barely a half-inch.

The creature shot through the opening, knocked the gate open, scurried inside the garden of #32 Milla de Oro and across the garden like a dog chasing a ball.

As the creature reached the front door of the home, that gate closed with a loud "clang!" It was the loud "clang!" that caught the attention of Paul Kanie, Roxanne and Stephon's bodyguard.

Paul Kanie had been smoking in #32's back villa. Hearing the gate, Paul grabbed at the handle of the pistol hidden beneath his guayabera and briskly headed to the front of the home.

The creature leapt from the ground to the ceiling of the home, disappearing from sight as Paul arrived at the front corner of the home. Paul saw Top-Hat and Ording in the Renault as soon as the gangster and the occultist saw him.

Ording whispered, "He sees us. The creature can flee in the streets. Get us out of here."

Top-Hat whispered, "Why? There's no law against parking a car."

Watching the car, Paul glanced down the length of the home but saw no one. Knowing there must be accomplices to the criminals in the car, Paul whispered, "Where are you, you bastard?"

On the roof, the *die schädel* crawled to the back of the home, reaching the ceiling above Roxanne and Stephon's bedroom.

Paul took two steps away from the building, in an attempt to see the top of the home.

In the car, Top-Hat asked, "Why isn't that bastard in a trance?"

Ording said, "He must not have been in the house!"

Top-Hat commanded, "Put him in the trance now!"

Ording whined, "I already told the creature to get the kid! I can't switch up commands! It doesn't work like that."

Top-Hat hissed, "This is why you bastards lost the war. You can't think on your feet."

From the roof, the *die schädel* reached down and

grabbed a window sash for the window to Roxanne and Stephon's room. The creature pulled the sash, but the window wouldn't open.

Paul had insisted all the windows and doors be locked tight during the night and siesta.

The creature pulled again. The window wouldn't budge.

In the front of the house, Paul listened, trying to hear anything unusual.

The creature rolled onto its back and hummed so softly it could only be heard by the boy in the room directly under him.

Stephon Gracia opened his eyes and sat up in bed. The young boy didn't know why he suddenly opened his eyes. The young boy didn't know why felt the need to finally give in to the urge he had all day, the urge to run outside on the grass.

The young boy turned to face the side of the bed and moved to put his feet on the floor. He silently walked outside of his room, down the hall, and stood at the top of the stairs.

Outside, Paul walked across the lawn of the home, his eyes up at the house, looking for open windows or any place a thief would break into.

Inside #32 Milla de Oro, Stephon took a step from the landing onto the first step of the stairs. A small creak wheezed from the step. Stephon took another soft step, and then another, not slowly, not fast. There were no other loose boards on the staircase, no other steps that would wake up his mother . . . until Stephon reached the last step.

Paul reached the far side of the home, having crossed the front yard. The bodyguard glared at the windows on the side of the building, looking for any openings.

As Paul walked to the back of the house, Stephon walked down the stairs.

The creature, on the roof, was reaching the limits of its powers.

The officer in the kiosk blinked twice and realized he was daydreaming. Taking a good look at Milla de Oro, the officer asked himself, "Who owns that Renault?"

Paul said to himself, "To hell with this non-confrontational B.S." and headed for the Renault.

Stephon reached the first floor. The board in the living room floor let out a huge groan that roared through the church-like silence of the living room as he stepped on it.

Roxanne shot up, half awake, her arm grabbing instinctively for her son.

In the Renault, Ording gasped, "Something's wrong. I can feel it."

Top-Hat glared hate at Ording.

Roxanne jumped out of bed.

Stephon opened the front door to the home and stood in the doorway.

Roxanne bellowed, "Paul!"

Paul turned, saw Stephon standing in the open doorway, and ran towards the boy.

Stephon had taken his first step outside.

The creature jumped from his hiding place, down to the boy.

Paul pulled his gun and shot a single shot at the creature, the most he could fire before the creature grabbed Stephon. The shot missed the creature and buried itself in the wall of the home.

With Stephon under one arm, the creature darted towards the fence, crawling like a spider. Inside the home, Roxanne ran out the front door, arms and legs pumping. Paul attempted to grab the creature but was knocked down by the monster's animal-like strength.

Ording flung open the door of the Renault and commanded, "C'mon!"

The creature reached the gate and jumped straight up and over the wrought-iron fence with an impossible leap. The creature landed beside the Renault. Ording pulled his creature inside the car.

Top-Hat threw a paper envelope from the car onto the sidewalk as the car drove off, disappearing around the corner in seconds.

In the kiosk, the officers blinked out of the trance and officer growled, "Oh no. Oh, Culo. Oh no, Culo."

CHAPTER 25

THE KIDNAPPING OF STEPHON GARCÍA SET OFF A SERIES OF events.

It was 1952, Madrid, Spain. Thirty seconds after the Renault pulled away from #32 Milla de Oro with Stephon García inside, the officers in charge of guarding Milla de Oro called for assistance on the police radio. It was too late; the boy and his kidnappers were gone.

The officers pleaded for leniency to the Police Chief and then to the Mayor. Officer Lorenzo, the officer who awake but frozen by the *die schädel's* mystic powers, pleaded his case. "It was a spell-caster! One of those bastards from the war!"

The Mayor told Lorenzo to shut up.

Sweating and shaking, Mayor Jose reported to Dictator Franco, "A boy has been kidnapped from Milla de Oro."

Franco bellowed, "Transfer all those idiot police to guard a horse stable in Soria!"

"Very good, sir!"

Franco bellowed louder, "Tell S.I.B. to fix the situation!"

On leaving the dictator's office, the mayor breathed a sigh of relief, happy to be alive, happy to leave the problem with S.I.B. Hearing they were to be transferred to stable duty and not executed, the officers from Milla de Oro breathed a sigh of relief.

Five minutes after the Renault pulled away from #32 Milla de Oro with Stephon García inside, Roland felt someone violently shaking him and bellowing the words, "U ave to out for hear!"

Roland realized he was hungover and not hearing correctly. He muttered, "Jesus, please be cops and not gangsters."

Roland opened his eyes and saw his only friend, Petey the Fence, standing over him. Roland looked around and realized he had fallen asleep in the back-room of Pete's Thrift Shop.

Roland muttered, "What?"

Petey replied, "Stephon has been kidnapped."

A wave of terror filled Roland's every cell, and the confused drunk stuttered, "I didn't do it."

Petey said, "It doesn't matter. The boy was taken from #32 Milla de Oro. Caudillo Franco takes crime on that street personally. Every criminal in Spain knows not to screw with that street."

A slack-jawed Roland asked, "What am I going to do?"

Petey said, "Hop in my car, in the trunk. I'll drive you to the Puerta Del Sol. I have a friend that works on a steamer. We'll get you on that."

Roland nodded his head in agreement. Petey didn't mention that it was the Apaches that had set up Roland's smuggling out of Madrid. The Apaches wanted Roland gone, because Franco's people always suspected the husband first in kidnapping cases. If Roland was gone, the authorities would look for Roland. And, if they happened to find Roland, the cops would waste hours making him confess to a crime he didn't commit.

Ten minutes after the Renault pulled away from #32 Milla de Oro with Stephon García inside, the incessant crying of a baby woke Stanley the Snitch up from his alcohol-induced slumber.

Stanley the Snitch was sleeping in the St. Charles houses, a government funded housing development that had fallen into disrepair. The incessant crying of an uncared-for baby wasn't unusual on the St. Charles houses, but as the crying woke Stanley, the petty-criminal and informant thought, *That kid is crying longer than usual.*

Stanley rolled off the couch and stumbled to his feet, still wearing the same clothes he had thrown on yesterday afternoon. Stanley faltered over to his apartment door, which was ajar. Stanley looked at the door and thought, *I must have left this open when I came in.*

The half-drunk Stanley was shocked into something approaching sobriety when he saw a young boy being ushered into the room next door.

Stanley could see perfectly into the hallway, as it was lit by a bare-bulb. The youngster that caught the eye of Stanley was obviously not a resident of the St. Charles houses. All the children native to the St. Charles' houses looked tired, exhausted, ill-fed and neglected. The child being ushered into the room across from Stanley's flat had the look of a boy who had spent the majority of his life being cared for.

The young child was being rushed into apartment 5c.

Standing in the darkness of his apartment so he couldn't be seen, Stanley the Snitch realized, *This is the type of info Mr. Brett pays for.*

Eleven minutes after the Renault pulled away from #32 Milla de Oro with Stephon García inside, Stanley the Snitch called Mr. Brett for a very informative 30 second call.

Twelve minutes after the Renault pulled away with Stephon García inside, Mr. Brett got a call from Mayor Jose, demanding he take care of the situation at Milla de Oro.

Mr. Brett was investigating the hotel room of Berhtram

Braun, S.I.B. informant that had gone mad, when the calls were forwarded to him. Before leaving the room, Mr. Brett grabbed a photo I.D. that had been separated from dozens of others by Mr. Braun.

Twenty minutes after the Renault pulled away with Stephon García inside, Mr. Brett was at #32 Milla de Oro with a squad of S.I.B. agents. Kidnapping was a serious crime in Madrid, and Mr. Brett wanted to operate out of the child's mother's safe-space when tracking down the criminals.

CHAPTER 26

When Mr. Brett and his caravan of enforcers arrived at #32 Milla de Oro, the home was a hive of activity by the victims of the kidnapping. Meera the Sardincian and Roxanne O'Brien, the kidnapped boy's mother, were reading the ransom note. Ms. Perez-Sanchez was screaming at Paul Kanie, the security man that lost the boy.

It was 1952, Madrid. Mr. Brett arrived in the front of three cars, each filled with S.I.B. agents. The agents were huge, close to two hundred pounds, and the epitome of fitness. Their perfect physique had been formed from their years of training in the Regulars de Cuenta, a division of the Spanish Army based in Morocco.

Mr. Brett walked into the living room, followed by his

squad of Regulars. The soldiers shut the front door, blocking it, when the armed group were all inside the villa.

Andrea Perez-Sanchez stopped berating Paul when the soldiers entered. Ms. Perez-Sanchez had met Mr. Brett on an earlier occasion and knew his reputation. Concern flooded into Ms. Andrea Perez-Sanchez as the lawyer knew Franco's government would cover-up a kidnapping if the crime couldn't be solved. The lawyer also knew some cover-ups involved making all witnesses, including victims of the crime, disappear.

Mr. Brett smiled and said, "Hello. Terrible situation we are in. I hope and pray that I can count on your support to see a positive resolution."

A nervous Ms. Perez-Sanchez stated, "Of course."

Mr. Brett quickly replied, "Thank you so much. Are you going to introduce your friend?"

Ms. Perez-Sanchez paused for a few seconds, her trained analytical brain going through every possible reason a government official would want to know about Meera the Sardincian. In the end, Ms. Perez-Sanchez admitted that Mr. Brett was no ordinary bureaucrat so the lawyer just stated, "This is Meera."

Mr. Brett smiled and said, "A pleasure to meet you, Meera. It's always a pleasure to meet a Latviarian, my mother was from there."

Meera replied, "I'm not Latviarian; I'm Sardincian."

Unsurprised, Mr. Brett replied, "My apologies." Feigning a confused look, Mr. Brett then started another lie. "On an unrelated note, a young man had been running around town, claiming to have some Kannakannack tobacco."

Meera exploded, "The bastard! Where is he? That's my tobacco!"

Andrea rolled her eyes in frustration, not wanting to believe that Meera had told Mr. Brett everything he wanted to know without the S.I.B. investigator asking a single question.

By the time Ms. Perez-Sanchez was ready to whisper "Be quiet!" to Meera, Mr. Brett had already taken out a photo I.D. card, the card Berhtram Braun had pulled from dozens of others. Mr. Brett handed the card to Meera and asked, "Is this the man that stole from you?"

Meera said, "This is him! This is the rat bastard!"

Interesting, thought Mr. Brett, *If I can get this hillbilly to ransack the monk's apartment thinking it's the thieves and wreck any dark magick spells he has before my guys go in, that would be excellent. If the tobacco is actually there, great! If not, who cares?*

Mr. Brett said, "I have information that he's staying in a monastery. For political reasons I can't send officers in."

Meera growled, "Where?"

Mr. Brett asked, "In exchange for telling you where the

tobacco is, could you do me a favor?"

Meera cautiously whispered, "What?"

Mr. Brett replied, "There should be a mirror in the room with your tobacco. Would you smash it? If you are uncertain which mirror it is, smash all you come across."

Meera agreed, "Certainly!" Meera didn't ask why Mr. Brett wanted the mirror smashed. Meera didn't care.

Mr. Brett pointed to a Regular and commanded, "Drive her to Las Descalzas Reales." To Meera, Mr. Brett said, "His apartment is in the back, third floor, second window in, across from the stables. You'll have to sneak in."

The group watched Meera rush out the door of Milla de Oro.

When Meera was gone, Mr. Brett turned to Paul Kanie and said, "Would you care to help me out? Stephon is in the St. Charles' houses, Apartment 5c."

Neither Paul, Andrea Perez-Sanchez, or Roxanne O'Brien asked how Mr. Brett knew where Stephon was. Over the years, all three had learned how large the S.I.B. informant network was.

Paul rushed out the door, followed by two S.I.B. agents.

Mr. Brett turned to Roxanne O'Brien and Andrea Perez-Sanchez. The S.I.B. agent said, "I'm assuming the kidnappers have called or sent a letter asking for money and a place to drop the money off."

Her eyes red and complexion pale, Roxanne held out

a piece of paper. "They threw this out of the car as they pulled away."

Mr. Brett took the paper. An address and the words, "*Jomhuri-ye Eslâmi-ye*" was the only writing.

Mr. Brett said, "I will take care of meeting the kidnappers."

CHAPTER 27

Paul Kanie and a towering S.I.B. agent stood out-side the gates of the St. Charles Housing Development. Another S.I.B. agent sat in an Erbo B45 van a half-block away, protecting the truck from being stolen, parked as close to the housing project as he dared. Inside the gates that surrounded the twenty-six-story buildings was a dangerous no man's land filled with plywood sheds and lean-tos, each makeshift building home to a dangerous man.

It was 1952, Madrid. Paul Kanie, an ex-boxer turned bodyguard, was looking for a kidnapped boy. A tip indicated that the boy, Stephon García, was in apartment 5c of Building A of the St. Charles Housing Development.

St. Charles had been built by the state, abandoned by

management, populated by half-mad squatters, and become home to gangs and thieves. If anyone was to disappear inside the development building's walls, their deaths would never be reported.

The S.I.B. agent, a former Army officer in the Regulars de Cuenta, looked at the number of possible adversaries in the field in front of him and asked, "How sure are we that the boy is here?"

Paul said, "Let's go," and walked through St. Charles Housing Development gate and to the St. Charles main building.

In apartment 5c, locked in a walk-in closet with a bare light bulb and a RCA Victor AM radio, Stephon García listened to government-sponsored pro-Franco propaganda on the public channel. The constant wailing of a baby from an adjacent apartment threatened to drive the young boy mad.

In the sitting room of 5c, two low-level Apache soldiers were on prisoner-watching duty.

Paul and the S.I.B. agent raced into the lobby of building A, then raced up the fire-stairs to the fifth-floor landing.

The fifth-floor stairwell door was propped open with an old shoe which had been stolen from its owner years ago and become communal property of the building. Paul peeked through the opening of the door, ready to grab his revolver.

The hall was strewn with litter. A drunk was passed out at the far end of the hall. Paul heard the wailing of the crying baby. He signaled for the S.I.B. agent to follow him.

Reaching 5c, Paul stood on one side of the door, out of sight of the door's peep-hole. The S.I.B. agent stood on the other.

Paul banged on 5c's door and shouted, "Hey, shut that kid up, will ya?"

Inside the apartment, an Apache jumped up to answer the door. The youngster was eager to use his new position in the Apaches to push the residents of St. Charles around.

The Apache flung open the door of 5c and bellowed, "Who do you think you—"

The youngster's words were cut short as the army-trained S.I.B. barreled into the room, tackling the boy and pinning him to the ground.

The second Apache stood stuttering, unable to believe that anyone would attack an Apache safe room. Paul ran towards the boy, shouting, "Don't move, don't move, don't move."

The Apache yelled, "He's in the closet! He's in the closet!"

Paul opened the closet door.

Stephon looked up and exclaimed, "Paul!"

Paul smiled and said, "Time to go home."

CHAPTER 28

MINUTES AFTER BEING INFORMED OF THE LOCATION OF her missing tobacco, Meera was outside Las Descalzas Reales Monastery, sitting in the passenger seat of a Pegaso Z-102. In the driver's seat was an agent for Spain's occult control squad, a former Regular de Cuenta in the Spanish Army, who whispered, "Third floor, second window in, across from the tables. Think you can make it?"

It was 1952, Madrid. Weeks earlier, Meera the Sardincian had a very valuable duffle bag of Kannakannack Tobacco stolen from her. Minutes earlier, Meera had made a deal with Spain's Social Investigation Brigade, Division M. The Regular repeated the arrangement. "You can keep your duffle bag, if it's there. Get the mirror and smash it."

The Regular held out an Ace of Spades playing card.

Meera nodded her head in understanding and took the card. She realized, *If they're asking me, a stranger, to do their dirty work, then they are afraid. They don't know exactly what's in that room.*

Some type of spells. Does the S.I.B. have their own spell-casters at work? Some type of protection against whatever is going on in that room? Or is whatever in that room on its last legs, and its magick is fading?

Meera shrugged, deciding that the various possible dangers were just something she would have to live with and exited the car.

Meera quickly crossed the street, entered the back monastery gate, and was in the alleyway between the monastery building and the stable. Meera walked down the alleyway until she was beneath the second window.

She kicked off her shoes and put the playing card between her teeth. A quick jump, a pull-up, and Meera was on the second floor. Getting from the second floor to the third was tricky, but Meera had climbed the Kannakannack Mountains since her youth. Meera's fingers found the gaps between the red-brick of monastery walls, her toes found spaces in the mortar. In a minute, Meera was outside the second window on the third-floor.

The window was a casement-type window, made up of twelve small panes forming one larger pane. The window opened on hinges, the same as a door, and locked with a lever. Hanging onto the wall with one hand and her toes, Meera took the playing card out of her mouth, stuck the card in the crack between the window and window frame, and lifted the lever from the closed position.

Meera pushed the window open, grabbed the inside window-sill with one hand and then the other. Having a firm grasp, Meera lifted herself into August Ording's dorm room.

Meera didn't get into the room unnoticed. An old man, unable to sleep during the afternoon siesta, was walking down the side street. Meera had been hidden by the stable for most of her journey, but the old man paused by the mouth of the alleyway just as Meera was climbing into the window.

The Regular in the Pegaso watched the old man, dreading that he would have to take some action to keep the old man quiet.

The Regular saw the old man happen to look up, the look of surprise on the old man's face when he saw Meera's skirt disappear into the third-floor window, and the look of resignation appear on the old man's face. The agent could almost hear the old man frustratingly mutter, "Can't even trust a priest these days," and happily watched the old man toddle away.

In Ording's room, Meera saw the bed, the chest of drawers, a sink, a mirror, and a duffel bag. Her duffle bag! With a feeling of disbelief, the Sardincian ran across the small room and opened the bag.

It's here. It's all here, Meera realized. The realization that her quest was over, Meera looked around the room, determined to fulfill her bargain with the S.I.B. She needed to find a mirror.

Meera looked under the bed, saw a pair of slippers. Meera ripped the thin sheets from the bed, pulled the pillow from the pillowcase. Then Meera moved to the chest of drawers, starting at that bottom drawer.

In the bottom drawer was a dusty bible, but other than the bible, the drawer was empty. The second drawer had some clothes. The second drawer from the top was more clothes, socks, and underwear.

The top drawer had the magick mirror—the mirror that kept *die schädel* bound to August Ording. Meera grabbed the mirror.

Under Madrid, in one of the hundreds of tunnels that crisscrossed underneath the city, the *die schädel* creature sat upright.

Meera threw the mirror out the window. Seconds later, she heard the crash as the mirror smashed into a hundred pieces.

Quick as a rabbit, Meera was out of the monastery window and on the ground, carrying her duffle bag the entire time. Reaching the Pegaso, Meera hopped inside.

"Let's go," Meera told the Regular.

CHAPTER 29

THE *DIE SCHÄDEL*, THE OCCULT CREATURE THAT HAD ONCE been the man named Thadeus Martin, blinked its eyes twice and stumbled. The creature fell forward, stumbling in the dark and landing on what felt like damp ground.

It was 1952, in the tunnels beneath Madrid. Confused and feeling as if had just woken up from a deep sleep, Thadeus heard someone shouting, "Get up! Get up, you stupid useless bastard!"

Thadeus couldn't recall where he was or how he had gotten into the dark tunnel. He asked himself, *Was I tied down? So someone could tattoo me?*

Thadeus heard August Ording again command, "Get up and get moving!"

Thadeus obeyed the voice, waiting until his strength and memory returned to fight back.

CHAPTER 30

JACQUES WAS COMING HOME FROM THE DIVE-BAR Micheal's, where the dregs of society were buzzing with rumors the Apache Top-Hat had kidnapped a child and was demanding some type of occult amulet as ransom. When Jacques opened the door to his apartment and heard rustling in the kitchen, the S.I.B. informant wrongly assumed the noise was his boss and muttered to himself, "Brett must really want to hear the latest!"

Jacques strolled into the kitchen and said, "Usually you're just taking up space on my couch, but do you have to eat my food?"

Jacques was stunned when he saw the Luger pointed at his chest. Petey The Fence growled, "I'll eat whatever I want, talisman-boy."

It was 1952 in Madrid. Jacques Proust knew being an informant was a dangerous profession, but he never guessed Petey the Fence would be the person saying to him, "Looks like I figured out your little game, Mr. Too-Good-To-Drink-With-The-Regular-Folks."

Jacques instinctively lied, "I don't know what you're talking about."

Keeping the gun trained on Jacques, Petey lectured, "Bet you're wondering how I figured out you had something important. How dumbass Petey the Thrift Store jerk figured out how Jacques had something everyone else wanted."

Petey continued, "I got a friend, a nanny that comes into the store every day. Always looking to buy or sell some crap. She tells me some story about how the grandmother of the kids she watches got swindled by some fly-by-night preacher."

"I says to myself, 'That sounds like a scam the Apaches would think up.'"

"This nanny keeps talking. She says the old lady thinks she was mesmerized! Well, then I knew the Apaches had some new scam thought up. Those French bastards are godless satanists."

"Then I remembered the first time Roland screwed me over. At Weymouth. We were supposed to sell a talisman for a lot of money."

"Roland talked a lot on those days. How after the war, we were going to have a lot of money. How the stupid piece of crap medal he was going to sell would bring us big money, because the schmuck buying it thought the stupid thing helped some mind-controlling demon."

"Then I remember how much you drink with Roland."

Petey paused in his speech, giving Jacques the chance to lie, "I don't know what you are talking about. I don't have a medal or badge or whatever it is you're talking about."

Petey reached behind him, pulled the *Jomhuri-ye Eslâmi-ye* Talisman from behind the small of his back, and growled, "Clowns like you always hide stuff in the tank of the toilet or behind the stove."

Jacques felt all courage leave him.

Petey commanded, "Turn around."

Knowing he couldn't argue with a gun, Jacques turned around, praying Petey wouldn't shoot him in the back.

Petey snarled, "Rumor has it that Top-Hat is waiting for some policeman to hand this thing over at the warehouse drop. When I give it to Top-Hat, I'll be the Apache's right-hand man. I would have left already, but you showed up. Almost caught me by surprise."

Jacques stuttered, "Hey, hey, don't do anything hasty."

Petey knocked Jacques in the back of the head with the handle of his gun, knocking Jacques out. As Petey left the apartment, he snarled, "I want you alive. So I can make your life miserable when I'm a top dog."

Chapter 31

Inside the abandoned warehouse was the gangster Top-Hat, the occultist August Ording, the *die schädel* living weapon, and a squad of Apache Crime Family soldiers. Top-Hat held a US M3 .45 ACP submachine gun slung over one arm and repeatedly murmured, "I hold all the cards. I have the kid, the creature, the guns. That *Jomhuri-ye Eslâmi-ye* is as good as mine."

It was 1952 in Madrid, Spain. The criminal Top-Hat had kidnapped Stephon García earlier. As ransom, Top-Hat demanded the *Jomhuri-ye Eslâmi-ye* Talisman. The talisman was a mystic occult amplifier, capable of increasing the hypnotic abilities of the *die schädel*. Top-Hat planned to use the amplified powers of the *die schädel* to strike everywhere and anywhere uncontested, to hold the people of Spain under constant threat of violence, to hold even Caudillo Franco in fear, unless Top-Hat was constantly paid.

Outside the deserted building where Top-Hat had marshaled his criminal forces, special agent Brett of Spain's Social Investigation Brigade parked his Pegaso automobile. Mr. Brett watched the outside of the warehouse, observing a few civilians wander past the building.

Inside Mr. Brett's left pocket was an Astra 680 revolver and in Mr. Brett's heart was the overwhelming desire to protect his beloved Spain from all dangers.

Mr. Brett took two deep breaths and calmed himself, knowing he had to go to meet Top-Hat and knowing he may not return. "At least we should have the boy," Mr. Brett muttered, trying to convince himself that his associate's mission to rescue Stephon was successful.

Mr. Brett picked up the two-way communications radio in the passenger seat beside him, keyed the radio, and asked, "You ready?"

Three blocks away, hidden from the gangsters inside the building, was Mr. Charles and a platoon of soldiers from the Regulars de Cuenta Division of the Spanish Army. Mr. Charles replied, "We are."

Mr. Brett and Mr. Charles knew how dangerous the *die schädel* could be. That the *die schädel* could mesmerize Mr. Brett. Mr. Brett had five minutes to leave the building with Top-Hat and convince Mr. Charles that the *die schädel* was dead. Otherwise, the Spanish soldiers would rush the building from the street and from the tunnels underneath the building. Mr. Brett knew that in the rush, there would be a very good chance that he would be killed by either the Apaches or friendly fire.

Mr. Brett didn't have the *Jomhuri-ye Eslâmi-ye* Talisman Top-Hat wanted. Mr. Brett had a cheap fake, a medal fabricated by one of the three old-man blacksmiths that lived on the edge of Madrid. The fake *Jomhuri-ye Eslâmi-ye* had rough edges and was covered in scribblings that to a semi-literate blacksmith looked like Arabic but to everyone else looked like graffiti. Mr. Brett wished he had time to take the rough fake to a jeweler and have the bronze hunk of metal smoothed into something that looked authentic, but there had been no time.

Looking at the fake *Jomhuri-ye Eslâmi-ye*, Mr. Brett admitted, "Not even a five-year-old child would be fooled by this. Thank God the actual *Jomhuri-ye Eslâmi-ye* is hidden far away, in the apartment the Apaches don't know about . . ." Mr. Brett's voice trailed off as he saw Petey the Fence, a criminal so low-level and useless even the Apaches didn't want much to do with him, hurrying down the street.

Over the radio, Mr. Brett asked, "Charles, the civilian, that one that's hurrying, you see him?"

Mr. Charles responded, "Sure do, but can't grab him

without making our presence known."

Mr. Brett had been an officer too long to believe in co-incidence. Mr. Brett knew Petey the Fence would do anything for a buck. He had to stop Petey the Fence. The agent sprung from his car and sprinted toward the thug.

Petey saw Mr. Brett charge towards him and bolted for the door of the building where the Apaches had grouped.

Chasing after Petey, Mr. Brett imagined Top-Hat inside the building, laughing at him, knowing that the S.I.B. agent's plans had started to fall apart.

Mr. Brett was inches from catching Petey when the door to the warehouse swung open and Petey dived inside. Mr. Brett followed, landing on Petey's legs. Dozens of hands held him, grabbed him, and punched him, pulling him upright. The hands reached into his clothes, pulling his gun from him, his two-way radio, his fake amulet.

After a moment of disorientation, Mr. Brett realized he was facing Top-Hat. The agent was being held immobile by a dozen arms. Top-Hat was smiling, the gangster knew he had won. The fake amulet was thrown on the ground. The gangster had the real *Jomhuri-ye Eslâmi-ye* in his hand.

Top-Hat growled to Mr. Brett, "I left you alive, because I want you to know how badly you failed."

Mr. Brett asked himself, *How long did the beating take? Thirty seconds? Two minutes? Four?*

Dramatically, Top-Hat walked over to the *die schädel.*

The creature was slumped against a wall. August Ording, the creature's caretaker, stood next to the creature, a smile on his face.

Mr. Brett thought, *The crazy magician probably thinks the gangsters will share some of the ransom wealth with him. Fat chance of that.*

August held out his hands to receive the amulet. Top-Hat growled, "Get out of the way. I'll do it."

Mr. Brett prayed, *Ording, you coward, show some backbone. Show some backbone. Argue for five minutes, you coward.*

August did not argue. August just backed away from the creature.

Mr. Brett took one last look at his situation. Surrounded by Apaches, the *die schädel*, Ording, and Top-Hat in front of him, Mr. Brett hoped for a miracle.

At that moment, Mr. Brett noticed something no one in the room saw. The eyes of the creature weren't the glazed over eyes of a somnambulist. The creature's eyes had awareness.

He's awake.

With a dramatic flourish, Top-Hat dropped the *Jomhuri-ye Eslâmi-ye* over the head of the creature and around its neck, held in place by a thin chain.

Top-Hat stood up straight, looked at the creature, pointed at Mr. Brett, and commanded, "Destroy."

The creature hissed back, "Certainly."

A look of terror exploded on August Ording's face when he heard the creature speak. In the next second, expressions of terror exploded on all the Apaches' faces. Mr. Brett was thrown to the ground. He heard windows shatter, the door to the warehouse kicked open, the Regulars de Cuenta charging into the building, a smoke grenade exploding. Then, Mr. Brett lost consciousness.

Chapter 32

Mr. Brett woke with the sun shining on his face, sore and bruised. There was a bitter tinge in the air as the acrid smoke of the gun battle faded away. Mr. Brett was aware of the lights from the ambulances that helped the injured.

It was 1952, Madrid. The battle between a group of Army Regulars, a squad of gangsters, and one occultist was over.

Mr. Charles leaned over his friend. As Mr. Brett blinked his eyes and consciousness returned, a smile spread over Mr. Charles' face. "You made it through. Again."

Mr. Brett sat up. He was in the street outside the Apache warehouse.

Mr. Charles explained, "Most of the criminals didn't make it. Top-Hat is dead."

Mr. Brett asked, "The occultist?"

"Dead."

Mr. Brett asked, "Petey the Fence?"

"Alive."

Mr. Brett asked, "And the creature?"

"Alive, but barely."

Mr. Brett got up and walked over the stretcher the *die schädel* was lying on.

Looking into the creature's eyes, Mr. Brett said, "Thank you."

Life was leaving the creature. He looked back at Mr. Brett and whispered, "Mary?" Then Thadeus was silent.

CHAPTER 33

A WEEK AND A HALF AFTER STEPHON HAD BEEN RETURNED to his mother, Mr. Brett made a series of visits. Mr. Brett loved to wrap up loose ends, and wrapping up the loose ends to what he called "The *Die Schädel* Affair" gave the bureaucrat pleasure.

It was 1952 in Madrid. Mr. Brett walked into Andrea Perez-Sanchez's law offices and was quickly shown into Ms. Perez-Sanchez's private room. Mr. Brett saw the concern on Ms. Perez-Sanchez's face, and thought, *Can't anyone even think for a second that I have good news?*

Mr. Brett told the lawyer, "Roland has been found guilty of conspiracy, by decree of Caudillo Franco. Any challenges to Roxanne's divorce are non-existent. The Apaches have been warned to leave your client alone."

Ms. Perez-Sanchez was very happy. Mr. Brett left and went to the office of Smithburg Office supplies.

Mr. Zack Smithburg had been let out of prison, as Mr. Brett's investigation into occult artifacts had concluded. Mr. Smithburg's company had been given a huge contract to supply Madrid. Zack rehired Stacy Gomez, Mrs. Gloria Sanchez, and Roxanne O'Brien.

Mr. Brett had bought the sackful of Kannakannack tobacco from Meera for a tidy sum, and the Sardincian had returned to her country.

The last person Mr. Brett chose to visit was Jacques Proust. When Jacques entered his apartment, Mr. Brett was sitting at Mr. Proust's kitchen table, enjoying a coffee.

A huge smile spread over Jacques' face when he saw Mr. Brett. Jacques was looking forward to leaving Madrid, to getting away from Micheal's, to going to bed early, and not having to see criminals.

A smile spread over Mr. Brett's face as well. The government official extended his hand. The men shook as Mr. Brett said, "Great job, my friend! Great job."

Jacques was beaming with happiness. Jacques' happiness spread when Mr. Brett pulled an envelope from his briefcase and handed it to the French-American.

Jacques opened the envelope and was stunned at the amount of cash inside.

Mr. Brett said, "The Caudillo sends his best. The entire operation started to catch thievery, but we caught so much more."

Jacques said, "I'm glad it all worked out."

Mr. Brett said, "Thrilled you feel that way. The next operation will be even more successful."

Confused, Jacques said, "Next? I'm leaving for America in two days."

A faux-confused look appeared on the face of Mr. Brett. "Leave?" the S.I.B. official asked. "I didn't know you had your passport."

Jacques stuttered, "I thought that is why you were here."

Mr. Brett shook his head and forcefully said, "No."

Realization flooded into Jacques. *They aren't letting me leave. I'm too valuable an asset.*

Mr. Brett got up to leave. As Mr. Brett exited, he told the defeated Jacques Proust, "Enjoy yourself! Madrid is a wonderful city that you will enjoy for a long, long time."

ABOUT THE AUTHOR

D. LEITRIM lives in BOSTON, MASSACHUSETTS AND HAS three cats. *Skulls in the Shadows* is his first book.